21
The Year to Blow Off Steam

21

The Year to Blow Off Steam

by CTL

I would like to dedicate the book to

" The wrong people on the right nights"

21 stories
about being 21 in 2021.

Table of Contents

BEGINNING

"**A**re you ready to begin?" the man said with a thick Irish accent.

"Is it going to hurt?" I asked.

"No," he said whilst flicking through a piece of paper with information on it. "Says here your name's Courtney... isn't Courtney a girl's name?"

"So I've been told, mate," I respond unamused. "Let's just get this over and done with."

"Talking helps some; how was your year?"

"Heavy," I respond.

"Ahh, to be twenty-one again," the man reminisced.

"I'm twenty-two now."

"A tough couple of years for your generation; I bet you were happy when lockdown ended, free to do as you please, go out, see your friends, go to the pub... talk to girls?"

I gave him a death stare and said, "I think I may have overdone it."

"Is that right? Go on then, give me a taste," the man said, fumbling through his bag in an uncharacteristically unprofessional manner.

"It all started with"...

1

CHAPTER 1

"THE FIRST SUNDAY AFTER THE END OF THE LOCKDOWN"

When twenty-twenty-one arrived, and the great Lockdown ended, I was shocked at the world I came back out to.

I mean, I had two birthdays in lockdown—nineteen and twenty. Those were some of your prime shagging and partying years, and they were gone. Erased.

Taken by some twat who ate a bat and a fat blonde Etonian wanker who had the cheek to tell us not to go out when he was getting smashed in Parliament, no less.

By the time it ended, many of my generation had grown up. We missed the twilight years from nineteen to twenty—the oh-so-necessary conversion therapy from teenager to adult. Many people came out mature, and some of us did not.

I was one of the many individuals who struggled. I had no idea that the world was filled with miserable wankers, pension plans, unstable rent, taxes, and LinkedIn. I didn't understand the colloquial language of brunches, council tax, work drinks, and early nights.

The ones that did learn how to swim in the deep end made the rest of us look like pathetic twats.

They were fitter; they had courier jobs, stable, steady relationships, no substance abuse problems, an affinity for brunch and, worst of all, they enjoyed working in the office.

They completely missed the point.

These were two prime years to develop habits that you spend the rest of your life attempting to get rid of, and they had done the complete opposite.

I wanted to have that thing that old people have when you ask them about the eighties. The classic nostalgic breath out coupled with a long stare into nothingness whilst saying dramatically, "Fucking miracle I'm even here."

I craved it, and a desk job wasn't going to cut it; I needed to fuck up poorly and make all the wrong decisions so I could tell my kids when they asked:

"Dad, what were the twenties like?"

I'd look at them and say, staring at my Tesla robot butler, "Fucking miracle I'm alive."

This was what was circling my mind whilst I sat at the cinema watching *The Unbearable Weight of Massive Talent* starring Nicolas Cage as Nicolas Cage.

I'm stuffing my face with gummy worms whilst watching the shitty pre-movie ads. No one else in the cinema is watching them except me.

With every advert that passes, I conclude that I could do a better job. Cinematic shots of a handsome man driving a BMW play on the screen.

The bloke smiles into the camera, and the words "Freedom is an electric BMW away" appear.

"Pfft, that's fucking stupid," I can't help myself. All car adverts have one thing in common: they tell you nothing about the actual car. It's brilliant.

Advertising creatives discovered a long time ago that people don't care about the intricacies of the car; they buy cars based on pure emotion.

A wet dream for advertising.

Somewhere along the way in the last one hundred years, they just decided to give you cheesy lines and shots of the car driving in serene places.

The rest is history.

I imagined the pitch, the boardroom, and the sale: some young ad creative saying with complete confidence into a boardroom filled with expressionless old mechanics and executives.

"This car is about a feeling." The ad creative looks out the window for dramatic effect.

The execs follow his eyes.

He pauses and waits until the room is filled with silence.

When they feel like it can't get any quieter, he tells them the cheesiest, most generic line.

"That feeling tells you: escape, let go, breathe in, release, and drive." He nods whilst making intense eye contact with the top dog. "FREEDOM IS A BMW."

The creative orgasms internally, and the executives give him a standing ovation. Fucking hell, I need a new job.

I eat away the stress.

One, two, three, four and more gummy worms.

I will regret it; these probably have over three thousand calories in them. Calorie counting used to be an object of necessity since the most exercise I was getting daily was a short circular walk around an empty park and, consecutively, my room. But now it's just a very lame habit that has clung to my brain from lockdown.

Soll, my best mate, is expectedly twenty minutes late.

I text him: "Where are you?" and then turn my phone's brightness down as I hear a vague but distant "tut" in the background.

I "tut" back because the film hasn't even started yet, and who are they to "tut" me?

"DING DING!" my phone rings. "Fuck," I forgot to turn my notifications off, and now I deserve to be tutted. They do not "tut" back, the cowards.

Soll: "Ging to bey 3 mins."

Courtney (Me): "FFS" (for fuck's sake).

I know full well what "Ging to bey 3 mins" means. It means: "I am wasted and going to be a very late belligerent arsehole."

Being a belligerent arsehole doesn't bother me in the slightest.

However, the cinema is my sanctuary—man tears, encouraged snacking—and should be treated with respect.

The adverts end, and the movie starts. Thank God.

A belligerent drunk man stumbles in and says in a loud whisper: "COURT... where are you?"

It's Soll.

• • • • • • • • • • • •

The tutters "tut" and shouters shout:
"SHUT IT!" from the left side and "SHUSH!" from the right.

Soll stumbled around at the front of the cinema, trying to turn on his phone's flashlight. I couldn't see his face, but his body language insinuated that he wasn't sure if he was in the right room.

He leaned back and flicked one arm out—a bit like a camp zombie—and said into the small but angered crowd, flashlight on, illuminating his face menacingly, "Who said that?"

I knew that the two men on the dates were not tough as I had seen them outside, and they were built frail at best.

Knowing Soll was in no danger, I relaxed and ate more gummy worms.

He'd find me eventually, and besides, this was becoming an amusing scenario. Why not tempt fate for the amusement of the cinema?

Good idea.

I shout from my seat:

"SHUT IT!" trying my best to camouflage my voice by adding a cough at the end. People are now understandably trying to find the source of the cough for health and out of fear.

"WHERE ARE YOU!" Soll stood on a chair in the front row and shouted up at the mountain of cinema chairs in defiance.

Ducking down behind my chair, I emit a war movie-like monologue to give this moment drama.

"UNAWARE OF THE ENEMY'S WHEREABOUTS, ONE MAN STANDS ALONE.

AGAINST TYRANNY, HATE AND PEOPLE TRYING TO ENJOY THEIR DATE."

• • • • • • • • • • • •

"WHO SAID THAT?"

"THE ENEMY IS ELUSIVE; THE HERO IS A PONCE."

Soll did not like people knowing that beneath his mockney

accent, brave fashion choices, and the large tattoo he sported, he was a wealthy Jewish boy and one of high pretension and effete.

I had struck a chord. "WHERE ARE YOU!"

The whole situation was getting out of hand. You could hear low grumbles from girlfriends urging their dates to do something about the drunk idiot.

You could also hear the low, grumbling replies from the men who just wanted to watch Nicolas Cage drive a Ferrari miserably.

Unbeknownst to me then, that juxtaposition held some weight in my life, too.

Soll, now angered, climbed over the first row of seats into the trench of the second. He flopped around near a family who quickly dispersed to the left and right before he fell forward, clasping at the headrest for support.

But he wasn't going to stop; he was on a mission now.

He looked like an unenthusiastic soldier in the First World War, not particularly eager to climb out of or into a trench.

Happily in no man's land.

After Soll had tackled the first four rows of seating, he stopped to reassess his flopping chair approach. It wasn't particularly effective, and any courage he had built to face the enemy had been thoroughly removed by tripping up every couple of seconds.

Between each row, he would say, "Courtney?" whilst whimpering in the dark alone.

I had to see this through. The film chimed on.

Just like Soll, Nicolas Cage was whimpering. He was doing it outside his hotel room, drunk and alone in the darkness. In contrast, Soll was whimpering in the darkness of an old Odeon cinema near Piccadilly Circus.

The difference was undeniably pressing.

Soll mustered up some more Dutch courage in the sixth trench. He knew the enemy was close.

Suddenly, he sprang up and began to run using the headrests as foot placements. Majestic idiot, how brilliant.

Without balance, half a brain and much alcohol, he was gaining momentum and making a direct beeline for my seat.

He jumped each row with such blind arrogance that it seemed as though God were assisting him.

Before I knew it, the drunken acrobat had arrived at the row in front of me, completely unaware of how brilliant his act of acrobatics was. He would only be able to reflect tomorrow in a state of severe hangxiety (extreme anxiety on a hangover caused by memories of the night before), unable to appreciate his successes.

Hands on hips, he stood before me, ready to confront the enemy.

I could now see he was wearing a particularly well-fitted beige Burberry trench coat, which is irrelevant, but it was disarmingly well-fitted.

At this point, everyone in the cinema was peeking over their chairs to see what the crazy drunk man would do.

But I knew Soll just like I knew myself; he was all talk.

"What's up, rabbi!" I said, revealing my identity and big grin using the light from my phone screen.

His face was disappointed; in his pursuit of the enemy, he had run into another idiot.

He turned to the cinema and announced:

"Watch your film, drink your drink, kiss your girl or boy or other—I don't discriminate—but there will be no fighting today."

Sighs of disappointment and frustrated "ughs" could be heard all over the cinema. He slumped down into the seat next to me.

They would only be getting what they paid for today—the greedy bastards. Soll reached into his trench coat and passed me a bottle of expensive-feeling vodka.

By expensive-feeling, it had that matte finish to the glass; it wasn't smooth like an Absolut; it was grainy, perhaps Grey Goose.

"Mr Low's is expensive shit, and it's in Mayfair, but I brought vodka," Soll stated as though this explained his reason for being late.

I nod and eat more gummy worms, my silence his approval.

Soll's and my friendship is based on a few things: outrageous disappointments to ourselves and our respective families, a nihilistic attitude toward the world and, finally, a profoundly misguided love for cinema.

Soll loved cinema because it was simple; within the seven meta-plots, there is order. It can never surprise you, no matter how hard the directors, actors and writers try. Once you have watched a comedy, tragedy, rags to riches and fame, a quest, a voyage, and a monster to tame, you cannot be surprised; you can predict the future; it is certain what will happen.

It's the screenwriter's job to try to trick you, and that's where the fun is.

There was one other thing our relationship was based on, too...

"Do you want a bump of ketamine?" Soll whispered to me like a guilty child.

"I thought you were taking a break?" I whispered back, having zero confidence in the statement.

Soll pulled out a sizeable modern key, one of those keys with holes instead of ridges—a key that led to a mansion—but most importantly, a key that afforded the wielder the perfect bump.

Soll grasped at his keys; he did not want them to jingle in the cinema. He put the key into the cinema-appropriate small-sized plastic drug bag and felt around with it. After about a minute of kerfuffle, I and everyone in this cinema heard Soll sniff loudly.

"HFFT!" and then wiped his nose on his shirt sleeve. He then offered out both hands to me.

One holding the baggie and the other holding the keys. Mine for the taking.

As the keys were transported my way, they jingled loudly, and Soll let out a nervous snigger.

I felt around the bag, crushing the powder on each side, then using the key as a spoon; I cornered a large amount, angled the bag so that gravity and the key were working together, pulled it out and sniffed loudly, too.

The effects of ketamine are not immediate; they creep up on you—a sense of relief fills your body, your problems seem to fade, and your equilibrium leaves.

Nicolas Cage was submerged in a pool on screen, still holding a whiskey glass. "Weightlessly submerged," Soll said in an American accent.

We both laughed.

Ketamine afforded everything Nicolas Cage said to come off as profoundly profound and intelligent.

Brilliant.

Ketamine also doesn't stay in your system for very long, about twenty minutes, which is also brilliant.

"Wait, that's not that funny, dude," Soll said, relating to Cage's on-the-screen alcohol problem.

"Do another bump."

"Yeah, it's probably for the greater good," Soll.

"Yeeeeaaaaaaaahhhhh," me.

"Yeeeeaaaaaaaahhhh…." Soll.

"Snort," me. "Snort," Soll.

And so on and so on.

We both relax and slip deep, deep into the dark, cushioned depths of a K-hole. A K-hole is when your brain goes to another dimension, your body goes limp, your mind hallucinates noises and sounds, and for about thirty minutes, you look as though you have had a stroke. Not pretty stuff.

At some point in the film, loud gunshots start ringing out, which rudely awakens both of us.

Soll looks over at me, but due to the visual effects of the ketamine, he looks like he's a mile away; he reaches out his arm and mouths something in baby language. "We shud ger?"

Through my one open eye, I can see he's frustrated that the words he is thinking are not the words he is speaking.

He slaps his face with a limp hand.

I understand from the look on his distressed yet relaxed face that the film is ending, which is bad because once the lights are on, we are going to be exposed. "We crawl…" I say, drooling.

Soll shakes his head in agreement.

I use all of my abdominal strength to push my head off the back of my seat so that my body is in the trench. Soll copies. We begin to crawl to the left side, and music paired with end credits explodes over our heads.

We must be at the stairs by now. I get up, swaying, and Soll follows, holding the scruff of my shirt. We resembled a proud centaur in appearance as Soll is bent over forward from lack of balance, and my upper body is leaning backwards with my chest puffed, and arms cocked at my sides. The ketamine at this point was at its peak, and whilst Soll shuffled forward, I stepped down the stairs with caution. Teamwork.

After a couple of steps, I opted for lunges. One step, good.

Two steps, good.

Three, four, five, six, seven, eight. Last step to ground level.

"FACK!" I fall forward, rolling my ankle. I would feel the pain tomorrow.

We now have earned the attention of the occupants in the cinema once again. Soll grabbed my hand and pulled me up.

We limped out of the cinema, two soldiers limping off the battlefield.

"What if we never did that first bump, Soll?" I ask, sobered from the bright lights, acutely aware of the pain pulsating from my ankle.

We couldn't even watch a film without fucking up or fucking around. "Are we fuck-ups?" I ask him.

Soll paused and thought retrospectively.

"The way I see it, you made that decision a long time ago; the worst decision you made, you made a long time ago. It was the first one; the lowest low is the first time you get high."

He paused and thought in terms of devil's advocate.

"However, if we look at our lives like stocks, we have compounded interest and large returns as we spent the last two years in lockdown. Building on this thesis, I think we owe it to ourselves and our generation to live out twenty-twenty-one as though it were two years in one."

This made perfect sense to me.

"Twenty-twenty-one needs to be fun, like Vegas fun."

"Vegas fun it'll be," I replied.

"When doing ketamine in public places, check for disability access before arrival." The man looked perplexed but not worried, which was worrying.

"What a lovely story."

He was not listening at all to me.

I shouldn't have expected anything else, considering, but I did think about saying, "You didn't listen to a word I just said."

But then I had a better thought. This was an opportunity to go over the year in a healthy, therapeutic manner.

"You want to hear more?" I said, grinning.

The man, now fumbling through metal drawers in the room and still not listening, replied.

"Sure."

"The next thing I did was go to a party. My friends and I called it"...

CHAPTER 2

THE "I DESPERATELY NEED TO HAVE SEX WITH ANYONE" PARTY

So, let's talk about the first post-pandemic party after lockdown. A rather large affair, an affair I had made a big deal of in my mind, one I had thought about almost daily.

I'll begin with the chronological order of how things typically play out. You arrive and do the dance. The dance is hugging and shaking hands with 20-odd people you really have no connection with or even like.

The dance is to keep up appearances and remain strongly connected to the powers that be. It's usually hugs for the girls, handshakes for the guys you like, and fist bumps for the ones you don't. So after you have done the traditional courting rituals, you would scan the room for a sneaky link or a drink, etc.

However, this was different. People approached one another with caution. We were all aliens to each other, circling and assessing one another whilst thinking the same things.

You look sick.

You look fat.

You look fit.

You look pale.

I noticed I was dishing out a lot more fist bumps than handshakes. Interestingly, however, the number of hugs increased. The strong bonds were stronger, the weak bonds non-existent.

Some things were the same.

Peep the pretty girls dancing, the drunk toffs, that one guy that always has a film camera, the loud, obnoxious socialite, and my personal favourites—the stush aspiring rappers and producers near the DJ decks. They're my favourite because they always have their back up against a wall whilst they judge your dancing, whilst also simultaneously trying to articulate their own unique struggle from pen to paper or laptop to beat.

In the kitchen, I can see many girls who wish they were supermodels or influencers taking countless Instagram pictures and performing choreographed TikTok dances in and around luxury furniture and art.

I decided that both groups were relatively annoying. I surveyed the rest of the room in the hopes of finding someone or something that looked vaguely interesting to occupy the time between sobriety and drunkenness.

I usually feed an artist's ego or talk to a bricklaying guy. Or my absolute personal favourite: join the two groups and enjoy the mutual disgust.

I can see no bricklayers or artists at this party. Shame.

Ah, I see some friends standing by the fridge doing bumps off what I can only imagine is cocaine. Brilliant.

My previously mentioned associate and friend Soll ushers me into a bathroom to tell me some meaningless gossip about who has fucked whom during the lockdown and whether we'll be able to skimp our way into an event at a private members' club later tonight.

It's all so important in the short term and so irrelevant in the latter. My other rather moody friend, James, is smoking a cigarette, looking for anything or anyone in the direct vicinity to have sex with.

My friends have adopted a slightly camp and drunken way of talking to one another, very Russell Brand before sobriety, that is—swaying and flicking arms whilst using the name "darling" a lot.

We head to the bathroom. He begins to gossip, and my mind deteriorates as he talks.

"Soll."

"Jabari and Emily fucked."

"Soll, I don't give a fuck. I came in here for drugs."

I pull out my bag of ketamine, and he pulls out his bag of cocaine. We mix them on a marble toilet stand and create two massive lines. Before we consume them, we hear a familiar voice outside the door asking if he can get a line.

"It's fucking Greeny. He's always broke and never has any

drugs," Soll says.

I shrug and open the door.

Luckily for Greeny, the night is young, and we have enough drugs for now. So, we let him in with the hope that in the future, the same card can be pulled on him. Greeny is also my friend... unfortunately.

"Ello, ello, ello, ello," Greeny says in his best attempt at trying to imitate a geezer. Both Soll and I look at one another and take a deep breath, knowing we are about to dance.

"Ello, ello, ello." However, I add "sunshine" to the end of my "ello, ello, ello" to sound more authentic.

"What do we have here then?" Greeny says, knowing exactly what we have here. I lift my eyebrows in suspicion of his fake charm; Soll acknowledges my suspicion and shrugs his shoulders dismissively whilst dumping one-quarter of a gram of cocaine onto an iPhone Twelve. The screen flickers, and beneath it, I can see that Soll has three thousand like notifications from Instagram, a heart reply from a lady on Raya, and a notification saying Bitcoin is down five per cent.

Greeny's eyes dart between our faces and the pile of cocaine. He is trying to find an in.

I watch his eyes as he sees that Bitcoin is down five per cent and uses the information to make small talk.

Soll, as per usual, bites.

"You into crypto?" he says, knowing every young man on earth currently is into the get-rich-quick promises of crypto.

"Yeah, big time," Soll replies with enthusiasm.

"Crypto is his best personality trait," I reply whilst pouring one-fifth of a gram of ketamine into the cocaine powder.

The powders are distinguishable: cocaine is finer, and ketamine is shardy. Greeny, who naturally did not put any drugs down, pulls out his card.

"Allow me," he says, pulling out a Crypto.com card that gives you three per cent cashback for every purchase; I know this because I have the same one.

"I wonder how far we are away from racking lines with Apple Pay," he says.

He then pulls out an old-looking American note and rubs it between his fingers. "My mum used it in eighty-one; now I'm using it in twenty-one," he says whilst putting down a bottle of cheap prosecco next to the toilet stand.

"Cool, mate," I respond, thoroughly distressed by the fact that Greeny's family treats drug notes like family heirlooms.

We burst out of the door, and the first thing we see is three girls: one pale-skinned blonde with blue sunglasses and a lollipop.

The next girl has an afro peppered with rainbow-coloured hair clips and notably high cheekbones.

The last girl has a tight crop top, big pink Gucci sunglasses, gum, eyeliner, a slit in her eyebrow, olive skin and piercing pale blue eyes. She looks like Cherokee mixed with South American or something.

Her eyes say femme fatale in every single sense of the word. "You're scary," I say to her.

She looks up at me, smirks a cheeky smirk, chews her gum and brushes past me. I turn and look over my shoulder, trying to be casual; I fail at this. She and her friends laugh as they close the toilet door—presumably laughing at me and presumably on the warpath just like us.

The three of us walk back into the corridor with a certain level of camaraderie that one can only experience after you have done something bad together.

Onward we go, towards the fridge, which is housing our White Claw seltzers and where James is still chain-smoking cigarettes.

Soll and Greeny start to yabber and debate about how crypto is the future. I can faintly understand the conversation.

"China can't control it, but just wait until the United States makes their coin," he says loudly and utterly unaware of the fact that his crypto yabber is female repellent.

I see Ren, a party-related friend whom I met at a fashion event three years ago—also a way to escape this god-awful conversation. "Ren!" He turns and looks over, confused until his sight locks onto my hand, which is raised in the air; he tilts his head up in acknowledgement, then consequently sighs when he sees that Greeny and Soll are behind me.

It's too late to keep walking away, so he comes over.

"Long time no see, you good?"

"Yeah, I'm good," I say courteously.

Ren fist-bumps Soll and Greeny dismissively and without eye contact. He hugs James and gives him a wink. Bit suspect, but whatever.

Around forty seconds go by without either party saying anything, so naturally.

Ren says, "I'm going to go," addressing the awkwardness and unintentionally giving me a complimentary invitation to follow.

I follow but realise that because we haven't been going to the same parties for the last two years, I have nothing to say to him—like, nothing at all.

I attempt small talk, but it fails, so instead of talking, we sit in silence and roll up cigarettes, scanning the room for any way out of this awkward predicament.

Ren pulls out his phone, and I look across the party until my eyes lock on Greeny. He's around five foot seven; he has a weak jaw, somehow pale black skin, jet-black braids, bright green eyes and a long, angular face. He's awkward, just kind of uncomfortable-looking. He's messing with his T-shirt, pulling it down, ripping the collar and stretching his sleeves. It's a shame he's stretching his clothes because he is well-dressed—a modern kind of Kurt Cobain style. He looks cool, but it is unmistakably evident that he isn't comfortable. Greeny's dad was the drummer of a famous band back in the eighties. But unfortunately, his parents spent all their money on a lifestyle they could no longer afford. You could see some remnants of the high life remained in his composure;

he still had an attitude, clothes and an inherited drug problem.

To the left of an uncomfortable and inebriated Greeny, I could see the two individuals I had become particularly enamoured with during the lockdown. Soll, of course, still standing by the fridge stroking his somehow always sun-kissed bushy brown stubble and next to him stands a tall, handsome, dark-haired sociopath and very close friend of mine called James. They're not talking; they seem to be assessing how good the party is. After all, it is New Year's Eve.

Looking around this party, it seems that my list of acquaintances has risen, and my list of friends has shrunk. A symptom of COVID-19, or a symptom of growing up, I have no idea.

I walk over to James, who opens a pack of cigarettes that he's unwilling to dish out and shows me he only has one left. I take it anyway.

He nods. "Looking good, son."

"You too."

"You three," Soll attempts to chime in desperately.

We all let out a sigh in the form of exhaled cigarette smoke.

"So, Berlin Monday," Soll says in an attempt to change the subject. James responds by ashing his cigarette casually onto Soll's shoes.

An act so dismissive, and yet it so accurately summed up everyone's feelings toward the trip.

Soll, disappointed by our lack of enthusiasm, walks into the murky depths of the party, middle fingers cocked and aimed at us.

I can hear a clock, but I have no idea where it is coming from. "Tik tok, tik tok, tik tok."

I look at James and squint; judging from his reaction, he hears it too. He points up with his cigarette.

A large two-metre high, one-metre wide Keith Haring clock is on the ceiling. It's about to strike twelve on New Year's Eve. I can hear the distant cheers of other parties along the streets starting to ramp up as their hosts gradually begin to turn their music up, no doubt a symptom of increased intoxication.

There is a feeling in the air that this night is finally going to be different. I can see the anxiety in the room; the lingering feeling of worry COVID-19 has left on my peers' faces is slowly but surely dissipating.

Their anxieties are still written on their faces.

"How long do we have before another pandemic happens?"

"Who is still my friend?"

"Have I chosen the right party to go to?"

"Am I too drunk?"

"Am I still in love?"

"I wonder if anyone notices I put on weight?"

"I wonder if anyone can see I've been working out."

Worry, worry, drink, drink, celebrate.

I notice a change in the behaviour of the room. People seem to move frantically with a repetitive manner of drug breaks to the bathroom, small talk and phone checks.

They're either checking BeReal or Instagram to gauge how good other parties look and then checking Snap Maps to see how far they are.

No one in the room is present; they are so obsessed with seeing as many people as possible that they don't realise they have precisely that right now.

The clock strikes twelve. "Donggggg!"

Cheers erupt, and people come together for the first time in a long time, embracing each other with hugs, kisses, touches and all manner of sexual liberation.

I close my eyes, bend down and reach for a bottle on the table next to Greeny. I down it whilst watching Soll from across the room, who hasn't managed to find himself a New Year squeeze.

I smile at him and raise the bottle in a toast motion. He smiles, recognising the gesture and toasts me back.

I kiss one of the girls whilst thinking about the one in the bathroom. The girl keeps on staring at me, and I can't figure out why.

"Are you okay?" she asks.

Why wouldn't I be okay, I think, but the words don't come out.

"Are you okay?" This time, her voice sounds muffled, like shouting underwater. The feeling in my legs begins to numb out, and a cold sensation begins to travel upwards from my feet into my stomach, chest and then head.

The room is tilted; I am floating and falling.

I can see Greeny looking frantically at me. Soll is holding my head sideways, and James is screaming down at a phone.

I can't feel anything, but I know I'm tired.

Now on the floor immobilised, I look at the bottle rolled over to a piece of pink furniture where it stopped and stared back at me.

It's also Greeny's prosecco. Greeny just so happens to be an OxyContin addict, so I could be overdosing. I'm probably overdosing. I could let go. It feels like I could slip away.

But wait, there's something I haven't done yet. Say goodbye to my mother. No, that's not it.

All of a sudden, I remember a reason to stay conscious.

It spins around, circulating, keeping my heart going, my signs vaguely vital, my will strong, and my lungs still pumping air.

"SEX!" I half blurt out as Soll scoops vomit from out my mouth.

It's been too long, and I'm not going to die until that wrong is rectified many times over.

What a way to start the new year.

(Am I going to do the fade-to-black thing? Yes, I'm going to do the fade-to-black thing.)

It fades to black and then to…

The lights are bright in my room this morning, very, very bright, which is strange because I always manage to close the blinds before I hit the sack. No matter how drunk, I always turn off the lights and close the blinds. Another abstract thing about this morning is that it smells like an old person, and it's loud, which means that I forgot to turn the TV off. But the smell is unforgettable; you know, that kind of cabbage smell, or like mouldy biscuits.

"Oh, fuck, am I in the hospital?"

"Everything is going to be okay, Courtney," a sweet Latin voice says calmly. "I need a Latin girlfriend. Oh shit, did I say that out loud?"

I can hear some male laughter in the room. Great, I did.

I open my eyes to a doctor shining a flashlight into my pupil. I look from left to right as the blurs in the room turn from shapes to people, then to James, Soll, Greeny and my mum. Finally, I look at the doctor, and she asks me.

"Good morning, young man. Can you tell me the substances you took last night?"

I look over at James, and he shakes his head.

"I was stone-cold sober last night, doc."

The doctor rolls her eyes, and Soll and James leave the room whilst my mum shakes her head in tears.

I think I need a girlfriend.

"What hospital were you in?" the man asks again, writing more information down on a clipboard.

"Royal London."

"Is that your usual?"

"No."

He looks me up and down. "Private?"

"No."

He enjoyed that.

"And are you allergic to anything?"

"Distasteful comments."

He ticks a box. "Okay, carry on."

He's still not paying attention to the story.

"Right, where were we? The next thing I did was get the fuck out of England because it had been a while. We called it"...

CHAPTER 3

THE FIRST AWAY GAME SINCE COVID-19

There is nothing quite like a holiday in Europe to bring out the sad in lads, but we were determined to do it differently, and with the help of Soll's resources, we could.

I arrived at Heathrow to meet Soll, who had rented us two suites at a hotel at our destination. Greeny and James arrived twenty minutes later, and we started to prepare for battle.

Well, I say battle; it was a far more pathetic affair than battle.

Soll claimed his anxiety was acting up because Germany is close to Ukraine and Ukraine is at war.

"I don't deserve to die yet."

We all nod in agreement that twenty-one is a little early to die.

On the way into security, Soll, James, and I distanced ourselves by two metres from Greeny, who was fidgeting and scratching his arms relentlessly, either from opioid withdrawal or nicotine withdrawal. I still hadn't bollocked him for essentially making me overdose.

I looked at his helpless little head and decided to let him off the hook. He had enough problems to deal with without me giving him an earful.

So, instead, I got a couple of tinned G&Ts from a caviar bar and began the descent into a relaxed state of depravity. The boys joined in, and Soll pulled out a strip of Valium, asking us if we were:

"Allergic to flying?"

It seems we are all indeed allergic to flying.

There is a stigma around drinking and Valium that I don't particularly appreciate because if the desired effect is to have a drowsy, egotistical god complex, then mixing a G&T with Valium is a brilliant idea.

We boarded the plane disruptively. By disruptively, James and I literally had to combine both of our subdued intelligence to put a single carry-on bag into an overhead cabin. This delayed the plane ten minutes.

After a flight hostess told us off for being too drunk, we noticed that Soll was not with us. James peered over the seats and looked forward to the front of the plane. His face lost all expression. He sat back down and said nothing. I took it upon myself to look, too. I could see the tips of Soll's Jewfro sticking out in first class. He looked back and winked.

"He's flying first!" James shouted.

This didn't bother me, but James—whoa, it bothered James because James had the money to fly first. In fact, this was the first time in his life that he was forced to fly economy. Greeny and I felt little to no compassion toward this issue.

However, one good thing did come of it. James was now trying to outspend Soll; he bought us round after round on his dad's Amex, and then Soll bought us a couple of rounds on his mum's Amex.

"Do you know what's better than a silver spoon?" James asked rhetorically. "Go on, what?"

"A platinum Amex."

"God, James, you are a real fucking cunt," Greeny said to James jokingly. James laughed it off.

That was the general tone of the five-hour flight, lots of awful things being said out loud on a plane surrounded by people who were either listening because they hated what we were saying or laughing because they related. There were very few of the latter.

Once in the air, another group of drunk, almost identical Australian gentlemen loudly shouted across the plane at one another to make bets on who would win a game of cheat. Me or my fellow flight companion, James. We had become the in-flight entertainment for Queasy Jet Flight 212121.

They, too, were loudly saying equally obnoxious things about Amex and flying economy. This took some of the heat off us.

Then, there was a moment of calmness and silence on the plane. Dead silence. A silence interrupted by James obnoxiously shouting directly into my ear.

"I don't like Greeny; he's a seat filler."

I nodded, unsure of what James was saying.

Unfortunately, due to the Valium gin & tonic mix, he most likely heard James's statement and saw my nod of approval.

In fact, I am almost positive he heard it because he sat directly in between James and me.

Luckily for us, Greeny had taken eight Ambien and used around eight glasses of red wine (paid for by James's dad) to wash them down. Thus ensuring that anything he heard today, he would not remember tomorrow.

"A platinum Amex is the new silver spoon."

"I've been to Berlin; it's a lovely place."

In my head, I tell the man to stop interrupting my story. But in real life, I smile at him awkwardly and carry on.

In Berlin

Our hotel is called The Mandalorian, and it's situated in East Berlin. *YES, you heard that correctly... EAST.* However, I'm not going to lie. East Berlin is not a looker; it's grey, cold and slightly depressing.

In the day, that is, at night, the city comes alive.

Once we got settled at our hotel, we picked up only what I can describe as too many narcotics for four individuals to consume in two days. We had the drugs, and we were ready to embark on a journey. On this journey, we had hopes of getting to live out what every young man's fantasy is. Waking up in a hotel suite naked, surrounded by naked women, a face tattoo of sorts, torn furniture and Mike Tyson's stolen tiger. Yes, I am talking, of course, about *The Hangover*, and yes, every man, when they go on a stag night, has some part, some small, very prominent part of his brain that says:

"Let this night be the night." We were no different.

To start the night off, we laid out very large lines of cocaine on a glass table and began consuming them at an unhealthy pace.

"You feeling it?" Soll said, squeezing his nose with irritation and holding his head back.

"I feel weird," James responds, lighting a cigarette in our suite, which would inevitably make the room smell awful.

"I also feel weird," I exclaim, unsure why the desired cocaine dopamine high was not happening.

What would happen now, if this was indeed *The Hangover* plot, would be that Greeny the weirdo would have spiked us with Rohypnol, and then we'd spend the rest of the day looking for Soll.

We look at one another, unsure and bewildered, until I realise we haven't drunk any alcohol, and cocaine without alcohol is like being really focused; the focus was not what this holiday was about. To paint a picture for all of you non-drug-taking, law-abiding citizens out there, it's like drinking twenty espresso martinis minus the martini bit.

Cocaine is never the solution unless dissolved in alcohol.

The man was now paying attention to me. "Good."

I continued. "**THE NIGHT**"

So, after a lot of that, it's starting to get dark metaphorically and literally. We have no idea where to go; there are, of course, the obvious choices, such as KitKat or the Berghain. However, they turn down foreigners often, and in our current inebriated state, the chances of us getting into either of those places were thin.

In times of crisis like these, decisions are better made in environments that favour your chances of having a good night.

Soll was thinking; we were watching him think, thinking about what he was thinking.

"TO THE PUB!" he cried out.

"HUZZAH!", "HUZZAH!"

When going to battle, one must choose the appropriate armour for the terrain. Naturally, we assumed leather, camouflage, MDMA as the weapon, and French-speaking as the mode of communication.

We began to peruse the streets of East Berlin, searching in hope for some kind of pub, but on every street corner we turned down, we were met by the same evil.

Bars.

The reason bars are evil is simple: they lack ambience, and ambience is important. After a long conquest and a lack of energy to search further, we settled idly on what appeared to be somewhere in between a bar and a pub. We were nervous, unsure of what we were approaching. Was it a bar or pub, some sick mixture of the two, an abomination perhaps?

On the outside, this drinking tavern had no name, just two large factory windows, and through those windows, you could see nothing but the faint glow of candles lit and Germans talking to one another. We looked at one another and nodded in agreement that this was to be the place where the night was to begin. We waited nervously outside a sizeable rusty metal door that led inside.

Me, Soll, and Greeny lined up strategically behind the meanest and most German-looking of the group: James.

"Oh, for fuck's sake," he let out, realising that we were waiting for him to make the first move inward.

The inside was wooden, with old creaky floorboards illuminated by candles; the Germans sat on the pillows scattered on the floor; it was very bohemian. They drank and smoked inside freely. I imagine it was probably the sort of place the French Resistance would have celebrated in after blowing up some Nazi train tracks back in the war.

Discreet, authentic and rebellious. We walk to the bar.

"Four beers, please," James commanded with his back turned to the bartender. James would occasionally let out a nervous "So, the war, eh." Or "1945" as though it were a nervous tic.

The bartender was a tall, bald German lady with piercings on her nose and mouth; she was very punk.

She was not impressed with any of us.

"4 euros," she replied to the back of James's head.

"4 euros? What do you mean four euros, you silly goose? I ordered four beers." James patronisingly corrected her.

"4 euro."

At this very moment, James felt something that can only truly be understood by those who have grown up buying five to six-pound pints of beer in London. Every time you do it, you know it's wrong, but you do it anyway but here they understood us; they understood that the joys of alcohol should not be for the few, no, no, the joys of alcohol should be for the many, you should be able to get debauched off of ten euros, it is what God would have wanted.

James brought those beers back to the table, a fan of Berlin. We decided to forgive them for any past sins. A man that had just had the first taste of what Berlin had to offer. Freedom isn't cheap, but neither is beer in London. For the first time, we understood that in this tough and unkind city, there are pockets where things made perfect sense. We finished those beers and then walked back to get more beers, then to get shots and then shots and beers and then shots, beers, cigarettes and so on and so on until we were indefinitely and solely the only group of young men passionately shouting about how shit England is. We had become what every European country despises the most—the drunk British.

It was time to turn up from booze to what we had been told was the next step. It goes by the name of "Meow Meow", otherwise known as mephedrone. Ordinary individuals would shy away or perhaps proceed to consume mephedrone with caution. Not us. We went to the angry bar lady with studs in her mouth and smiles beaming from our faces.

"One more round."

We did so knowing we were being labelled the definition of the classic British tourist. You will understand this position if you have ever gone to one of the places where the British tourist was first officially recognised: Málaga, Tenerife, the Canary

Islands and parts of Ibiza and Spain. I was not sorry for the drugs consumed in the bathroom or, the drinks spilt, or the cigarettes smoked in elevators, but I can say with my whole heart that I am truly, truly sorry that Europe has to deal with English tourists.

She looked up and shook her head. James, frustrated, furrowed his brow in anger, but before his anger could burst out, Soll politely and softly said with an air of confidence in French:

"Je suis tellement désolé pour nous, c'est le dernier et puis nous sommes sortis." This translates to: "I'm so sorry for our behaviour; we will have one last, and then we're out."

We had the drinks; we had the mephedrone. Now, all we needed was the club.

After drunkenly asking people at the bar what they thought was the best club in the area with little to no success, we left.

Soll and James looked for cabs whilst me and Greeny smoked our cigarettes and finished our mephedrone-laced beers.

Mephedrone, not to be confused with methadone, is also a stimulant that makes you less socially aware and, to put it mildly, energetic.

For me, it was like removing distractions; you could see, hear, smell and taste everything the way you wanted.

Out of nowhere, Greeny, who essentially spoke never, asked me a profound question, one that had me thinking deeply about the night ahead.

He said, ashing his cigarette into some cold, windy Berlin air headed for my face: "Do you believe the night gets better after three am here?"

What a deeply profound question, one I had pondered often. Was this the land of the free where bagheads stayed up in unison gambling degenerately, calling in sick the next day and making awful excuses to their girlfriends about why they couldn't get their dicks hard? I replied sincerely:

"I don't know, Greeny, but I sure do hope so."

A cab was hailed, and Soll, in his imperfect French, asked the cabby what the best club was. It was clear to us that speaking English got you nowhere good in Berlin. The cabby said with a sigh of relief back to us in broken French something along the lines of:

"I thought you were English; good thing you weren't; I would go to the Anomaly Arts Club."

We all replied in drunken English, "To the Anomaly Arts Club," revealing our true faces and bad intentions in an instant.

We drove, and we drove through the dimly lit streets of Berlin, smoking our cheap cigarettes and drinking our "Meow Meow" in silence. Once in a while, Greeny, James, Soll or I would perk up and ask:

"You feeling anything?"

To which the reply would almost always be, "Maybe." We would later come to find that Meow Meow was a maybe drug. Maybe I'll try. Maybe I'll have another. Maybe sexuality is a spectrum. Maybe this is the best drug ever.

We all sobered up in the car ride, and the drug seemed to kick in; a state of calmness washed over all of us; we felt as though we were flying, soaring even; it felt like we were swimming with the current. Our newly relaxed state and Soll's surprising ability to speak fluent French meant we were able to get into the club with relative ease. James, Greeny and I kept our large, unfiltered gobs completely closed; we even smiled at the bouncers and meant it.

The club was like a hippie commune in both look and stature; cargo boxes lay scattered atop one another at awkward angles. One cargo box juts out and acts as the entrance, which is unguarded. Dazed ravers walked in and out of it, no doubt to be there for days or to finally leave after days. James walked through first, followed by me, then Soll and Greeny, who limped in behind us like a wounded gazelle. Once inside, things were not as they seemed on the outside. For starters, all the insides of the cargo boxes were cut out to make three distinguishable and very large domes, apparently all playing different music. However, all I experienced was a large mixture of techno.

"Everyone is in leather," Soll said in a tone that indicated fear.

"Does anyone have a cigarette?" Greeny responded, completely disregarding Soll's observation.

Out of the corner of my eye, I could see a cigarette machine that was illuminated by a psychedelic spotlight.

"Over there," I said, pointing casually to both let all the German women know that I was cool and that I had, like, "been here before."

Greeny walked over, leaving the pack to fend for himself; we kept moving to a place of safety for any group of lads ever scared and on holiday—a place where you go when your back's up against a wall; yes, we were back to the bar.

We ordered a round of gin and tonics, once again in French, to let any Europeans in the close vicinity know that we were friendlies.

Drinks drunk, cigarette lit, false sense of confidence and belonging acquired, time to dance.

How does one dance to techno? I'm not sure; I'm not even sure that Berliners know. We stood in a line like soldiers and assessed how we were to go about this particular ritual.

To the left of me was a large, presumably homosexual man in a ball gag, leather underwear, green fluorescent glasses and a pink beret. Side note: if he's not homosexual, he is very comfortable with his sexuality, and I would salute him for it. However, he tried to chase me around the dance floor for two hours, and that made things rather inconvenient.

Here are the tips that I observed from watching someone dance to techno:

1. **Plant feet.** This is important because you're going to want to have a good centre of gravity when you indulge in this highly cryptic, weird dance.

2. **Have sunglasses.** You don't want people to know your identity at all.
3. **Wear leather.** This is not a must, but it does increase your chances of fitting in, which increases your chances of people once again being unable to identify you.
4. **Flick arms out;** yes, you guessed it, as a defence mechanism to stop people who think they have recognised you from getting close and confirming that it is indeed you.
5. **Finally, the last tip is to pout;** I don't know why they do this, but from the evidence I have deciphered, it has more to do with being German than the techno thing, so I see it as optional.

I follow all my steps, and so does Soll; we are doing our crab dance, and something spectacular begins to happen; we become those guys.

Becoming one with the music, doing the weird dance, wearing neon sunglasses, sweating profusely with a leather jacket on and pouting vigorously.

The next step was to do this strange crab dance towards some females and see how that could go. We successfully found two Italian girls submerged in the smoke machine, blaring speakers and green lasers.

"What's your name!" I shouted into her ear.

She replied something in Italian, but it came across as "blah blah blah, do you have any drugs?"

I nodded and gave her some of our ecstasy; we both took it, me a little more hesitantly because of the mephedrone, cocaine and alcohol circulating in my stomach, creating a bomb.

But they're all uppers; let's go to the moon then. Plus, in 2021, if you give a girl drugs, you better be taking them yourself.

We badly danced and then said all the rather cringe, lovey-dovey MDMA stuff one naturally does when on performance enhancers like:

"You're different."

"I feel a connection with you."

To which she would nod because she didn't know English and it was very loud. To the right of me, the giant muscular homosexual man with fluorescent sunglasses started to crab dance towards me; I began to crab dance further away from the man and closer to the Italian girl in an attempt to make it very, very clear that I was straight. But at that moment, maybe just for one or two seconds, I looked at the man, and the part of me that gets off playing devil's advocate said, "DO IT." So he approached me and said something along the lines of "Hello" in German.

I looked him deep in the eyes whilst my heart thumped nervously and replied, "Hello" in English.

A look of disgust covered his face, and at that moment, I learnt lesson 16.

"Everyone hates English tourists, even large horny gay men on MDMA."

"I studied in Berlin," the man said, trying to find some small morsel of relatability.

"Oh yeah, what did you study, bartending?" The man laughed.

"When was your last injection?" he asked.

"Yesterday."

"Yesterday?"

"Yes, yesterday."

"You are aware that if your last injection was yesterday, you might be dealing with some serious health repercussions in the future."

"How soon?"

"How soon? What?" the man asked.

"How soon will the health repercussions come."

"A couple of years, a decade, we don't know, that's the point."

"Next week?"

"Probably not next week."

"Good, do it then."

He shook his head in shock, then pulled out four different cloudy fluids, placed them on the table and asked me to continue.

CHAPTER 4

NEXT STOP THAILAND

The next story I am about to explain is one that came about out of necessity; it is not one that I would have chosen willingly. Halfway through the year and a couple of months after Berlin, it hit me that I had reached a crisis point. I don't know what your limit is, but everyone has one, and mine was waking up next to a lovely seven-foot Jamaican lady in a small loft bed somewhere in Tottenham in a council estate with Greeny and no memory of what had happened. The estate seemed to be filled with sleeping heroin junkies. Greeny was lying in the one spot of the room where the sun was beaming in onto his chest and head, smoke puffing out of his mouth; I couldn't help but think how peaceful he appeared. A particularly precarious situation, I must say. If I'm completely honest, the Jamaican lady was around six foot three, and I didn't mind. The cuddle afterwards was phenomenal.

I had a problem with my heart, no, not soppy love issues.

As a twenty-one-year-old man, my heart is starting to do strange things in the morning, beating out of sync too quickly or too slowly. The lifestyle was catching up.

But on my glorious walk home, God, Allah, Jesus, Moses or one of the omniscient beings above sent me a sign in the form of a phone call.

I look down; it's Soll.

"Hello, sunshine," I say, croaking and spitting out the remnants of last night.

"How would you like to go to Thailand for a health retreat courtesy of my dad?... Well, I say courtesy; it's more like he's genuinely worried about our health?"

"Any man crazy enough to say no to a free health retreat in Thailand doesn't deserve to go to a health retreat in Thailand."

Getting to Thailand is no small feat; it requires a transfer flight through Dubai, and you have to sit on a plane for thirteen hours. Now, despite having many privileges given to me in my life, one I have never had before was a first-class flight. I know a guy who can send you Ambien from Mexico. You can then use the Ambien and a glass of red wine to have a first-class experience whilst still sitting in economy, but I have never physically sat in the golden forbidden helm, the place that separates those who are comfortable from those who are not—the first class—a place that shows you so clearly that you are living worse than the one per cent. Until now, I was going up in this world with two first-class Emirates tickets.

For Soll, this was the usual, but for me, it was clear; nothing could be clearer; this experience was going to be better than any secret club in Mayfair or even Soho. "Why do I make that comparison, I hear you ask?"

Four things make an aeroplane one of the better experiences you can have in this world.

1. The altitude means that the drink hits you harder, faster and smoother for all of my accounts.
2. You have free table service, and aeroplane hosts and hostesses care for your every need; tell me one time you've been at a club in Mayfair and been given a bread roll.
3. You are in a large metal cylinder that could be grounded at any moment by a rogue duck; your entire existence is at the peril of a duck; if you don't drink to it, drink because of it.
4. You have nowhere else to go; you have no distractions, no service, and no one to bother you; in all honesty, it might be the most relaxing part of your holiday.

Whilst waiting for the plane, we both took a handful of Valium, drank some free Moët and took advantage of the free croissants at the bar. We both knew this was the last time we were going to get to consume carbs for a long while. Naturally, we found two seats with a view of the airfield, and both sat and slowly sank into our chairs. The pairing of a croissant with the free Moët is almost as good as a cheese and cracker, or that's how it felt at the time. Anyway, during the hour wait, at some point, we both fell asleep and awoke to this:

"Can Soll Franklin and Courtney Bernard-Doe please come to the boarding gate? The flight is about to take off in ten minutes?" A large teleprompter voice bellowed.

The adrenaline of the situation overtook us as we both awoke wide-eyed and thinking, "Surely not?" Soll looked down at his watch and began sprinting to the airport gate. We were both entirely incoherent and began to fight with one another over the direction of the gate; however, after hitting each other in a manner only comparable to a T-rex. As we ran through Heathrow, the Valium hit Soll off his equilibrium and onto the floor, resulting in me tripping over him and falling onto a small Asian seven-year-old boy and mother. They were more upset about the fact that I accidentally removed her son's mask than the fact that I had hit him at full acceleration. The lady began to scream at me, and I looked up directly at her, expressionless, back still firmly against the cold Heathrow marble floor, and assessed the damage.

One must when dealing with the memory loss side effects of mixing alcohol with Valium.

You know who you are and where you are, but you don't know where you're going, and this became evident by the fact that Soll and I stopped at the four information desks on the way to our gate. We later discovered that there was only one information desk and we had visited the same one four times. After our fourth lap around the information desk, we decided to change tactics and began to think the way we knew best, with blind arrogance. I saw an airport buggy and ran over, holding a fifty-pound note in the air like a white flag as if to say I surrender.

He looked at me with a level of sarcastic astonishment as I explained our predicament to him.

"Soll is needed to fix the teleprompter at gate six immediately."

"Is your name Courtney?"

I replied, defeated, "Yes."

"Well, I've been looking for you; you booked a disabled cart an hour ago to gate six."

I looked over to Soll lying flat on his back still and then back at the driver, and with confidence, said:

"He is unfortunately a spastic."

To wit, the driver shook his head, looked at Soll and responded with a straight face.

"Don't you mean physically impaired?"

"Yup, that too."

We got on, Soll lay sprawled out in the back row, and I sat next to the driver; he told us to hold on, and I braced; the driver cracked his knuckles like his driving was going to be a strenuous activity. He hovered his foot above the accelerator, shifted the gear stick, pressed his foot down, and we were off; we were going fast for about ten seconds, and then he stopped.

"Why have you stopped?" I pleaded.

The driver smiled and pointed to the right smugly. I couldn't believe it. I laughed out loud, and Soll's discombobulated head sprang up from behind me; we were in disbelief. The sheer ignorance and idiocy that we managed to reach, even trying to complete the easiest of tasks, surprised me. It turns out we had been at gate six the entire time, which meant the Asian boy and mother were going to be on the flight. The help desk we went to was just the staff at the gate door, and we had been running in circles around a small duty-free Starbucks for around one hour.

But after all of that, the real kicker was that we had arrived at our gate an hour early.

We stumbled out of the car embarrassed and bought a few gin and tonic cans from the local duty-free and based camp near the gate, occasionally forgetting what we were doing and why until a nice Thai lady and small boy an hour later reminded us that we were on the same flight.

Valium and alcohol make for a great story you can't remember.

Silence.

"Do you smoke cigarettes?"

"When I drink."

He looks me up and down, checking another three boxes with ticks.

"When do you drink?"

"Three times a week."

"How many units?"

"Nothing massive, six to eight."

He gestures with his hand to continue.

The act is dismissive, but this whole interaction is dismissive. It's on brand, so I keep it moving.

"Right, right, so we get to Thailand for a:"

DETOX

I've heard that if you change your environment, you can change how you think; if you have ever tried psychedelics, you know this to be true. Once the airport doors open and you breathe in the thick, humid Thai air, you feel different. Within moments of looking at the Koh Samui landscape and up at the sun, you and everyone else who just got off the plane think to themselves, "Maybe England is just as bad as we say it is."

Whilst waiting to get past immigration, Soll and I assess an irritated Scandinavian family whom I can tell from their clothing, jewellery and surgery is going to the exact health retreat we are.

The dad is a great big, bald man with small round glasses and a big bulbous nose. He is wearing Yeezys, presumably not bought himself, as he looks ridiculous in them.

His wife is a ten in the kind of typical posh blonde mum kind of way. She's the kind of woman who's a ten because she can be; she has nothing else to do but work out, walk dogs and go to beauty salons.

Finally, they had a small daughter who was probably around

twenty. She had green eyes, a beautiful angular face, and mousy blonde hair. They were all wearing the most extra mask equipment I HAVE EVER SEEN; I mean, you'd think these masks would stop tear gas.

Soll is a mouth breather; he can sleep standing perfectly upright, head tilted to the sky, mouth gaping, breathing in and blowing out. Other than the occasional grunt of sleepy discomfort, he looks at peace.

Soll's mouth weapon was directly aimed at this family, causing them a great deal of discomfort. Without any warning, he walked over and said, "Put your fucking mask on."

We were scared, and we did exactly as told. Two dogs hounded by a wolf. On the way out of the airport, I saw a book called *Why the Scandinavians Do It Better*. I bought it. I can see how buying a book about his country could be seen as a compliment. But in my own way, this was a Machiavellian tactic. Use ingratiation to undermine your enemy. I explained this to Soll, still in a Valium haze from the flight. He looked at me and then at the book I had bought, then at the Scandinavian man who was still eyeballing us.

He needed clarification. I tried to explain to him my tactics. To wit, he replied:

"You've got issues."

"Probably."

But that's why we were here, to fix the issues and get a healthy body and mind. We both sat back and fell asleep, waking up an hour later at the gates of the retreat. We get out of the cab and hop directly into a golf cart driven by a monk type. The golf cart is playing meditation music. Manufactured chimes, hums and dings calmly play as we're pulled up hills, through caves, over beaches, dining halls and over the dunes near the sea.

Koh Tao Health Retreat is like a cult of healthy, wealthy people. The compound itself is walled off from the real Koh Samui with tall white walls coated in vines and shrubbery. The actual buildings and facilities are advanced treehouses. Each treehouse had straw ceilings and wooden planked floors. To the naked eye, these huts looked primitive, but looking closer, each treehouse had its own unique health-prolonging technology.

The facilities include a colon therapy centre, steam, dry and infrared saunas, two gyms, an IV drip section, chiropractors, various advanced Pilates-looking equipment that could be mistaken for sex restraints, Botox, lipo surgery, facelifts and on and on.

Soll was still knocked out, so I took it upon myself to slap him in the face multiple times.

"Oi!" I shouted at his face.

"What, mate, what?" He squinted, holding up his hand to stop the incoming sunlight from burning his unadjusted eyes.

I pointed at the guests. We were in disbelief.

Every single person in the compound was staring at us. People came out of their cabins, got up from their dining chairs and lifted their heads up from their outdoor massages to see us.

"Why are they looking at us?" I asked the monk type. He turned to us and said in broken English, "You young."

It was almost as if our age had ruined their experience; we had made them aware of their mortality.

Soll and I looked at them; besides a nice tan, an expensive smile and good clothes, these people were essentially polished turds. Beneath their happy exteriors was something else. If you looked for a little too long, you'd see glimpses, twitches trying to escape and reach the surface.

Fat old alcoholics struggling to make eye contact, plastic surgery junkies grasping to what youth they had left, and tech CEOs that had only ever chosen work instead of everything else. Many of them are too rich to stop drinking or eating better year-round. So, instead, they used this place for a week or a month. It was an expensive cheat code for life longevity.

The guests' interest in us waned quickly; it had been around twelve hours since Soll had consumed nicotine. Soll usually breathed in about as much oxygen as he did vape smoke, so this was a touchy topic. He patted around his body, frantically searching for his Juul stick, the one thing that could relieve his anxiety, the one thing that might make this weird place bearable. He patted his trouser pockets, then his shirt pockets, and then he searched through his Amiri knapsack. Then he looked at me.

"WHERE IS MY VAPE!"

Honestly, I had stolen it whilst he was passed out on the plane and then dropped it under my first-class seat when I passed out. I tried to get it, I really did, for like an hour, but then a lovely lady came by with a croissant, which distracted me. The anger in his eyes told me that I should keep this information to myself.

So instead, I said:

"You dropped it under your seat when you passed out."

He breathed heavily.

"Get me to the reception NOW!"

The golf cart drove on, winding around the cabins and tree-houses through the surrounding jungle. Armies of green birds flew overhead, squawking down at the squirrels who defended the palm trees by squawking back in another language.

We were headed to the highest point in the compound, a place where our hearts would be tested, and our health would be saved. The car came to an opening where the jungle ended, and looking around, you could see one large treehouse. This treehouse was not like the other ones; there was nothing primitive about it. Instead, it had electric glass doors, marble floors, a skylight and a chandelier. The monks were dressed in black instead of the traditional orange and white we had seen everywhere else.

We got out of the golf cart, which zoomed away quickly.

"Hello, Courtney, hello, Soll. Phones, please?"

We responded impolitely, but he smiled anyway.

"Phones, please," he repeated.

I handed mine over. Soll handed one over.

He led us to a room where we were meant to sleep for the night.

"Why can't we sleep in the cabin?"

He replied with some bullshit about COVID-19-19 and something about our chakra energy being so off it would disrupt the other guests. Whatever that means.

The room was primitive, with two hard bamboo beds and a fan that spun very slowly. I looked at Soll and lifted my eyebrows in a way that said this couldn't be worth ten thousand pounds. Soll passed out, and I watched the sun go down over the sea. A perfect pink-orange sundown fading over the horizon.

A NEW BEGINNING

An alarm rattled off at five am, the room spun as we both jumped out of bed to search and destroy the source.

Knocks on the door.

"Time for your tests." A small lady peeked into our room at Soll and me, completely alarmed.

We were separated and made to wear stupid robes and sandals and then sent our way into the big house to find out how bad the damage was.

Five hours of sleep, humid weather, no sugar, alcohol, nicotine, social media, drugs or screens of any kind.

This means these next thoughts weren't my greatest or best, but here they are. Our routines were given to us. We were to have thirty minutes of infrared sauna every day, one massage every day of varying techniques, no phone, no alcohol, no carbs and no drugs. All we were to consume was juice, vegetables and the occasional book. This was new territory, but if I knew one thing, it was this.

A lady pricked my arm to take my blood, tested my urine, felt my temperature, took my heart rate and asked how I was feeling.

"How do you feel?"

"Bad," I replied.

She giggled, probably. I was still half asleep.

After going into various rooms with various small Thai women, who poked and prodded me for information, I was ready to receive the results.

I'm sitting in a room, still dressed in a stupid robe with stupid sandals, looking at my stupid heart rate and stupid alcohol levels in my stupid body. It turns out that I was just as stupidly unhealthy as I believed. If I'm unhealthy, I could only imagine how bad Soll was.

To my dismay, the nurse told me that Soll had a staggeringly low resting heart rate of fifty to sixty beats per minute. To be clear, that's Olympian level. Mine, on the other hand, was above one hundred and five, which is similar to the average retired stockbroker. I decided then and there that she had taken the reading wrong.

I commanded her to run the test three more times, my frustration visible. Instead, she calmly held my hand and told me.

"Don't you worry. We can get it down within a couple of days."

Her face wasn't particularly pretty, but her eyes were bright and golden. They were so round, and they seemed to reflect all the light in the room. She could have been an alien attempting to disguise herself as a human in a good way. Regardless, it calmed my frustration when she spoke to me; her extended eye contact and sympathetic facial expressions gave me the impression that she could see everything. Especially what I was thinking. I slumped in my chair and smiled at her. I thought she smiled back, but on later reflection, I realised she just had a kind face.

Soll waited outside the patient's room.

"What's your resting heart rate?" he asked.

"Thirty-five BPM," which is the same resting heart rate as Usain Bolt's. Luckily for me, Soll was paying no attention.

He had already begun to break the rules.

He was looking at a girl's Instagram page with ten thousand followers. He smirked, looked up at me and showed me that the girl had sent him nudes.

"What do you think?" he said, knowing precisely what I thought.

"Yeah, decent, decent," I responded rather jadedly, knowing that I myself would not be able to acquire that type of girl without a blue tick.

"Ah, the sweet, sweet smell of envy."

I knew what to do; everybody knew what to do when someone showed you their crush on Instagram.

Scroll down and double-tap a three-hundred-week-old picture.

"TAP, TAP, your girl isn't even twenty in this picture, pal," I smirked at him.

"Why the fuck would you do that?" he said as he snatched the phone and unliked it knowing the damage was already done.

It didn't matter, though, because Soll had a blue tick, and a blue tick is like being gifted a golden halo. You are above everyone else; the powers that be have verified you, and if the powers that be believed you're worthy, well, maybe you were. A blue tick is a golden ticket; if it's used right, it can get you anywhere. Now, if you want top-tier girls in this world, there are two ways to play the tick.

1. Number one is obvious; you slide into their direct messages or the DMs. Unfortunately, however, if this is real life and you see a desired woman of the other sex, well, now you are just like the rest of us schmucks, and you're going to have to somehow show that you're verified without coming across as a douche.

2. Do not fear, though; you must approach with caution and confidence. The key is to get her to follow you; once she sees the tick, she'll second-guess herself, "He must be special?" But we know the truth. Anyhow, once she sees that you're verified, she will inevitably be hypnotised by a feeling of validation that someone who is verified is verifying her. I suspect that in fifty years, when we all have Neuralinks,

the blue ticks will hover above those lucky few, showing the rest of us how important they are to society. I don't advocate for it, but would I abuse it if I were given one? Absofuckinglutely.

Soll and I separated ways and began our health journeys.

My first appointment was demeaning, to say the least; before I explain the procedure, I will tell you the typical audience to give it context. It is a well-known and used practice, typically for rich French housewives, to get colon therapy twice a month to clean out their intestines of year-old faecal matter. Colon therapy is not like therapy, which I knew how to do. No, colon therapy for me was having two Thai ladies stick a tube filled with chlorophyll up my anus and then massage my head and belly whilst encouraging me to relax.

In terms of masculinity or pride, forget it; leave those things at the door. You lie on a bed sideways in a gown as a Thai lady inserts the tube while saying things along the lines of "good boy" and "let it all out". I told her to stop speaking. Instead, she carried on unintentionally saying condescending but ultimately kind words of encouragement. If you want to get the most out of the situation, you have to be fully relaxed. You have to relax as much as possible; I was not relaxed at all. It happened, and it was unpleasant, but you do feel healthier afterwards.

Soll, in true Soll fashion, was waiting for me to come out so that he could film and display to his hundreds of thousands of followers my discomfort. Lovely.

Soll and I toured the island dressed in ordinary clothes, which made us look very out of place.

Everyone in the compound was fascinated by the spectacle that was us. I couldn't blame them; I'm sure they were all thinking the same thing.

"How could these young men afford a place like this?"

"How could they skip the waitlist?"

"Who are they?"

But more importantly:

"Why would these young men need or want to be at a health retreat?"

For starters, we were walled off from any outside entertainment like bars, girls or jet skiing by massive flora-covered walls and a metal gate guarded by two heavy-set monks. Secondly, all (other than Soll's) had been taken and locked away in the big house, which meant no porn, social media, dating apps, YouTube or even Netflix. Thirdly, the activities were created for people who needed to be on vitamin IV drips (Keith Richards types), and to the naked eye, we were not those people.

After the colon therapy, or anus defamation as I liked to call it, I had to take an infrared sauna. I overheard a conversation between two women through the sauna wall. That convo went as follows:

"No, the Bin Ladens are misunderstood; they throw a party every year in St Tropez."

"Oh gross, I went to their last party in Monaco; absolute shit show."

"How long do you plan on staying here?"

"I told my dad that the toxins haven't left yet, so I'm thinking another month, just in time for après-ski in Gstaad."

They both giggled, and I began to sweat faster.

Later on, toward dinner, we were herded together to talk about our unique experiences. Soll and I were not shocked to find out that they were not that unique at all.

By the third day, all of the so-called bad toxins had left my body, and I started to get it. The sun was shining, the birds were chirping, and the sea was crystal clear. Soll and I felt a little better and decided that we would eat together on the beach.

A beautiful couple around the ages of twenty-five to thirty were taking pictures of themselves doing yoga poses on the beach. It didn't even bother me; I was changing.

We decided to have a conversation with them.

I went over to them to say a casual "Hello, my name is Courtney," but before I could, the shirtless man embraced both of us. He was around six foot five, covered in tribal tattoos, muscular and lean. His ethnicity was a mix of Caucasian and Japanese, a clean-cut Keanu Reeves-looking type.

His girlfriend was around five foot five, African American mixed with Japanese also; she had perfectly placed freckles, a lean torso, a lovely smile and essentially the perfect arse and legs. Suppose we're going by current standards, of course. She also had the most amazing hazel green eyes, which Soll nor I noticed until hours later due to being distracted by her, let's say, other qualities.

An advert for love. They had thick American accents, and they were both from San Francisco.

After a bit of small talk, the lady asked me, "What do you and Soll do outside of the compound?"

My mind had a flashback to Berlin where me, Soll, James and Greeny had consumed so much Meow Meow that we had taken on a Stephen Hawking-like appearance whilst we debated whether ketamine or cocaine was a better drug for taking on a night out.

But instead, I said something far better; I told her a half-truth.

"We travel around London on the weekends, and I work during the week."

This was an answer so ambiguous yet boring that there was no way she could be interested in anything else I had to say, which was perfect because very little of what I had to say was good.

I was correct, and she began to blather on about star signs. It didn't matter; her presence was so hypnotising that she could have been spitting directly into our eyes, and we would have asked her to continue.

It was splendid; the sun was shining, the view of the ocean was beautiful, and they were perfect. It felt like going on a first date; we were playing the best version of ourselves to impress them.

They asked what we did for work, and I told them, chest puffed,

"I'm a junior copywriter for The IMAGINE THAT Creative."

They had no idea what IMAGINE THAT Creative was, which bothered me as my bravado and sense of self-worth had begun to come from my silly little job title. I would have felt bad about it if I wasn't sitting next to one of the world's biggest trust fund babies. Whatever he was about to say was going to be utterly ridiculous. I was pleased when he told them:

"I'm an investor."

Now, anywhere in London, people would immediately know that if you're investing at twenty-one, you probably have been given a bunch of money from Papa. But here, they were a little confused by our age and gave him a chance to explain.

"What kind of investing do you do?"

Soll would change this depending on who was around. Sometimes, it was real estate; other times, it was stocks and bonds. But once in a while, and only on special occasions, he would pull out my favourite of all the trust fund baby dropout lines.

"I'm in crypto, NFT, that kind of thing." Oh, how wonderfully current.

I couldn't help but let out a scoff at how ridiculous the statement was. He had lost his family hundreds of thousands, investing in the stupidest coins possible. The worst thing is that I had lost thousands of pounds listening to his advice, so I was no better either.

Regardless, crypto is one of the easiest ways to say I'm a self-made millionaire and have no one even bat an eye. The stories are everywhere; you can get rich in a day if you buy this coin. It's all crap, and they knew it. So I changed the subject.

"I love being healthy, eating well and chatting with interesting people." They smiled at my flattery.

"But I can honestly say that if I had a fucking beer and cigarette, this would be ideal."

My English humour left them expressionless and confused.

Often, this is the case with sarcasm and Americans.

Everyone ignored me, so I pushed the thought deep down into the depths of my liver, where it would be locked away until a later date.

After more small talk, I noticed a pattern, the kind of pattern you notice when you work in an advertising agency where everyone is always pitching ideas.

Why was the couple so overtly complimentary about the compound?

"Aren't we so lucky?" the lady said, staring up at the sky. I imagined that up there, God was probably flipping her off.

"This place is beautiful, the people are beautiful, and the sea is so wet, and the sun is so hot." These two weren't the brightest.

"I love this place, and I love you, honey," the man said, and we cringed. I was going to say something demeaning or sarcastic.

An unhealthier me would have heard that awful line of dialogue and thought, that sounds suspicious. But this was a healthy me, and I didn't want to cast unwarranted judgement.

However, it did occur to me that Soll and I weren't the only ones telling half-truths. So I asked them politely.

"What do you do?"

They replied with one word I disdain more than any other, a word so foul that it was able to bring me out of my golden haze and smack me back into reality, a profession so foul and vacuous it made me sick to my otherwise healthy stomach. They told me they were "ASPIRING INFLUENCERS" hired by the owners for one day to show off their facilities. The curtains had been drawn, and I saw clear once more. I closed my eyes, pursed my lips, took a breath, and told Soll.

"We have to go now." He got up immediately, and we both walked away without saying goodbye.

"Do you know what they are?"

"Scum," Soll replied.

"No, far, far, far worse than scum; we just met two breathing adverts."

"When people question your legitimacy, always say crypto. 'Have you left the country in the last thirty days?'"

The man asked, fumbling around the small steel room.

"No," I responded.

He checked another box.

A bead of sweat began to form on his head.

"Is there a problem?"

"Read the names and tell me which one you've had before."

I point at the far left bottle. It's practically empty.

"It seems we are low on stock. But don't worry; my nurse is on her way."

"What nurse is around at seven am on a Saturday?"

"Ones that get paid to do more than one thing." "What happened after that?"

I could tell he was stalling for time now.

He walked around me, assessing my physique. He didn't need to do that.

CHAPTER 5

"BY THE LAST DAY"

By the last day, the happy haze had worn off. I was craving not alcohol, not drugs or nicotine; those things, it turned out, were not my true masters.

No, I was craving food; I would have cut off my pinky finger to eat a côte de boeuf. But every time I ordered normal food, they brought me detox food instead. I was so delirious I would eat it and fall asleep at the table. I was surrounded by Soll's family of six, but the sugar cravings were so intense I might as well have been alone.

It felt like my body was being carried by a spirit that just had enough strength to puppeteer me to my last session.

During a massage, the masseuse began asking me very personal questions like:

"How was your day?"

"Is this pressure too hard?"

"Can I get you some water?"

Questions that scared me.

I told her everything; they had finally broken me. You could call it a state of exhaustion; however, they call it relaxation. I was rolled in salt by two masseuses and put in a cocoon-like wrap of towels. I was in a chilli burrito. It was hot, really hot; I was sweating heavily. So I asked the lady:

"Water, please; where's the water?"

She looked me dead in the eye, adjusted my towel with her index finger so that it covered my mouth, and left the room.

I tried to wriggle a hand free, but they were firmly stuck by my side. I could see a figure in the corner of the room, sitting and staring. Shoulders stooped, naked, wet hair draped over red eyes. The figure was slouching with a big fat beer belly. I started to try and move harder, and I started shouting.

The figure slumped onto the floor and inched closer to the table; it was almost entirely out of my peripheral vision. I could not move. I could only see its feet dragging in my direction.

The bed began to move as it climbed up the left corner toward my head, and I could see it staring directly at the left side of my face, two centimetres away from my ear.

The thing climbed on top of my chest and stood up. I looked at the clock and closed my eyes. It had only been half an hour. My lungs were finding it hard to expand under the weight of its dark black feet. I tried to shake it off, but it had all the power.

"What did it want?"

"Was this a part of the session?"

I breathed quickly and fast, sweat pouring out of the towel and onto the floor. Familiar faces from home entered the room— blurs—and they were trying to shake the thing off of me, too.

I got a hand loose, fell off the bed, and turned around to see it was gone. I ripped off the salty towel and drank some ice-cold water. The cold filled every corner of my body, and I headed for the pool.

I walked directly to the closest pool and belly-flopped into it. I welcomed the cold. When I emerged, I realised that I was directly in the middle of a water aerobics class. Around ten white country club-looking, seventy-year-old women were scowling at me. I had disrupted their synchronisation. I quickly turned and climbed out of the pool. My ears were blocked by the water, and I made a run for my room. As I ran, the staff smiled and waved. No one is that fucking happy.

I scurried up the hill toward our lodge, dodging the compound's happy helpers and subdued guests with the agility of an elephant on ketamine. I got into my room, closed the blinds, turned on all the lights, and hopped in a cold shower. I sat in that cold shower until Soll came back.

After thirty minutes, he arrived, laughed, and then said in a rather unfriendly manner:

"Pull yourself together. Dinner is in an hour."

After five days of detoxing, Soll and I were not speaking. It seemed the things we had in common had been stripped from us, and all that was left was a mutual feeling of exhaustion and pain. If we had dreams of getting girls to the compound, they had been stripped by a lack of libido. For the last five days, we just woke up, did our sessions, ate very little, lay in the sun, swam and slept. I was instructed to take my last infrared sauna before dinner and then a flight home. The saunas were at the bottom of the hill, and dinner was at the top. Dinner with Soll's dad was at the top. After the sauna, that hill was now a mountain. I looked up at the behemoth and asked myself:

"Can I do it?"

The pilgrimage began; there was a bamboo assistance bannister, which I held onto as I trudged up, reminding myself to breathe in the humid Thai air. Once I reached the top, to my dismay, it seemed that Soll's father had become close friends with the Scandinavian man who hounded us at the airport. They were eating together.

The German man looked at me with disdain and said, with a pronounced Scandinavian accent:

"Nice of you to join us."

It was nice of me to join them; it took much effort.

I looked like a rabid runt, smaller, weaker, but with crazed hunger. I felt deranged, my hair sticking up from the humidity, my skin thirsty, my eyes red, and I had nothing left to lose. I didn't care if he was a wolf and I was a dog; I was going to bite back this time. I sat down with my head drooping as my mind went in and out of delirium.

The waiter came over and asked me what vegetarian meal I wanted.

"Steak with potatoes," I muttered under my breath; this was no time for grace or decorum.

The waiter enthusiastically tried to remind me: "Steak isn't on the detox menu."

The big Scandinavian man asked me to repeat myself. So I did, this time whilst directly looking at the prominent bald doctor sitting across the table from me.

My pupils dilated, my breathing thick, my shoulders and neck slumped. He couldn't tell me what to do; I wasn't there. I looked through him; he was a big red blur, a bald blur.

"Did I stutter? I want a steak and potatoes, waiter."

The waiter politely reminded me that I had chosen the detox menu; if I had chosen the "Bulk" option, I would have been allowed to eat carbs and meat.

I put my head down on the table and closed my eyes. I woke up to steak and potatoes. The Scandinavian man had given me his food as he was bulking. "I guess the Scandinavians do it better," he said, reminding me of the book I bought at the airport.

We all laughed, and I tucked in.

The steak was overly well done, it wasn't seasoned, and it wasn't even good meat, but my God, I have never had a better meal in my life.

Everyone does it better than the Brits.

"You should count yourself lucky; if you were in Thailand right now, well, let's just say we'd be having a different kind of conversation."

"I'd be in jail, and so would you. How long is the nurse going to be?"

"Twenty minutes max." He sat down.

"Next?"

BANGKOK AIRPORT

I reached the airport and was happy that I wasn't flying with Soll. It was best we took a break from each other before being back in London.

How do you fill nine hours in Bangkok airport?

Well, it wasn't easy. The airport was massive, and it had one long strip that led from one side to the other, a straight walk that had to be at least a mile long. The walkway was patrolled by armed Thai police wearing heavy-duty masks, gloves and hairnets. They looked more like armed dinner ladies than police, which, in its own way, was far scarier. All the stores were boarded up by white planks of wood except the essentials: a Gucci store, a pharmacy, an off-licence, and a Subway sandwich stall. Rome was built on less.

I decided to hit them all. Gloriously. I skipped around the off-licence, carefully choosing a bundle of cold beer. Would I have a Cobra, or would I have a Shangri-La? I was going to have both; what a world. I bought the highest nicotine vape you could buy, and then I skipped to the pharmacy, smiling gleefully at the journey ahead.

"Hello, my dears," I said to the lady pharmacist.

At this point in the journey, I had had about six beers and was listening to this weird podcast about Sherlock Holmes.

Somewhere in the madness of this airport, I had become Sherlock, taking on his strange way of walking, alcohol abuse, and gentlemanly talking.

She looked up, unsure of what I was saying.

"I am in quite the pickle, you see. I'm terribly afraid of flying, and I need some Valium and Ambien, or I don't think I'll be able to bear the journey."

"Prescription," the lady bluntly replied.

"Right, yes, but of course, give me a moment."

I surveyed the shelves behind her for other alternative medication, just as I imagined Sherlock would have done. I couldn't understand any of them.

What would Sherlock do?

He'd probably Google what the next best alternatives were.

Search bar: *What medication can I get over the counter in Thailand that is anxiety-reducing?*

A bunch of stupid adverts came up, so I went to the place we all go to when you want to find out things you're not supposed to.

Reddit.

Reddit search bar: *What drugs do they sell over the counter that allow you to get fucked up in Thailand?*

Bigtitmonster438: Zoloft.

I swaggered back over to the counter, now armed with the information of every degenerate on Reddit.

"I need Zoloft and melatonin, my good dear," I asked, and she provided.

Bada bing, bada boom, and we were off.

I had proved to myself that I could detox, and now I was going to retox. I bought the vape, put my backpack on the floor near the gate, and began drinking.

Somewhere along the way, I took a Zoloft and blacked out.

I came to find out why this Zoloft drug was so coveted. Zoloft does this: if you have had six beers and a Zoloft, you've actually had fifteen beers. After around twelve FaceTime calls with friends in London and New York—I can't remember—I boarded the flight and passed out.

When I woke up to an old lady staring directly at my head in horror, which was resting against the chair in front of me, a puddle of drool had been compiling on my grey Nike tracksuit bottoms for about eleven hours. It looked very suspect. Still drowsy and frustrated from my trip, I passed through immigration. The officer looked at my passport and back at me, still drunk. It was evident we shared a mutual disappointment that I was re-entering the country.

Reddit.

"How often do you go out?"

"Often."

He ticked some more boxes on his clipboard. "Tell me more."

He put all the cloudy fluids into a safe near the door, then pulled out a bottle of ethanol and placed it in front of me.

"After the airport, I decided to continue to..."

CHAPTER 6

"RETOX"

21
21
21

Soll flew into London two days later and sent an emoji of a square into our Instagram group chat. This means he wants to go to an expensive club.

It seemed Soll hadn't scratched the itch yet, either. He wanted a RETOX too.

Everyone replied in a matter of seconds, which only bolstered our energy to take the night as far as possible.

I was going to invite some girls, Greeny was going to get a bunch of drugs, James was going to find a live fight, and Soll was going to sort out a table at a fucked-up club.

We met at a pub in Camden called **The Rhinoceros King**.

A dingy Irish joint with two pool tables, cheap Guinness and a barman who allowed you to do as you pleased. So long as you never broke a glass or talked about England in a positive light. That was fine; we took our pint glasses seriously, none of us were patriots, and James was half-Irish, so the owner put up with our shenanigans.

We talked business around a low-lit pool table.

None of us is any good at pool, but this was about serious business, and no place is better for conducting serious business than a pool table in a pub.

"Fights require the best stuff, pure Peruvian," James said whilst scrolling through the plethora of drug dealers he had on WhatsApp.

Greeny hit the cue ball, and it rolled slowly toward the eight as James reeled off drug dealer names.

"Crazy Pete."

"No," we replied.

"Cole West K."

"No."

"Jamal East."

"No."

"Jamal South."

"No."

"Pablo Northwest."

"Maybe."

"Pablo Nos."

"Definitely no."

"Pablo Crack."

"Fuck no."

It appeared that drug dealers love the alias Jamal or Pablo. Proper creative stuff. This went on for about ten minutes until he stumbled across a number he had acquired from a rich Brazilian guy we met at a weird burlesque club a while back. His name on James's phone was: **"Fat Bald Latin Man with Good Coke"**.

He read out the name, confused and unaware of what he was saying.

He corrected it, "Colombian cocaine man." One must be politically correct even when buying cocaine these days.

Now, the reason we were getting pure Peruvian is simple. Fighting is a sport where cocaine is consumed; it's everywhere. No, really, try and take a piss at a boxing or MMA event; the men's bathroom is a symphony of snorting, coke shits and loud, obnoxious shouting, mostly asking, "WHO'S GOT MY KEYS?"

It is everywhere, it's in the air, it's in the eyes, and it should be up your nose. I honestly believe a Tyson Fury fight at Wembley would give a Colombian coke shipment a run for its money.

James texts dealer, dealer arrives, and drugs are acquired. Back to the pool table for the next item of business.

"Down fifth pint and head to Bellator fight."

We all neck five pints each. The alcohol went straight to my head, and my brain went simple for forty minutes. Here's what I can remember.

I waddle outside the pub, buy cigarettes, order a cab, drop my phone on the wet pavement—it cracks—decide I don't care, pick up my phone, wipe off the grimy water, realise it's raining, flick my cigarette in the general direction of Greeny, laugh when it hits his forehead, look perplexed at horrified bystanders watching, say things along the lines of "I love you" to the pretty bartender on the street, fall on James, Soll orders cab, do a bump of coke to sober up, smoke another cigarette, get in the cab, pass out, wake up at the bar in Bellator stadium.

Pure Peruvian for fights, the bog standard for your average nights.

We got to the fight, and we downed two Jägerbombs each and then walked to our seats four rows away from the cage. We were very close, but the visibility was shocking.

Looking around the Bellator stadium, you could see rows upon rows of geezers, Essex lads, aspiring fighters, toffs, Londoners, Northerners, Southerners, casuals and un-casuals. There was even a bit of gender diversity scattered amongst the crowd—the odd miserable girlfriend, mum, aunt or hooker.

We had all placed bets on Fabian Edwards (UFC champ Leon Edwards's brother) to knock out his opponent. He walked into the ring, sweat dripping, the arena silent, the lights fixed on his ring walk, calmly composed, unaffected.

They circled each other, testing and prodding weak spots. Touching gloves, poking stomachs, punching heads, kicking hard, and bleeding a lot. Modern-day gladiators, gruesome stuff, primal but fucking entertaining.

Then it stopped. Fabian hit him in the jaw, and his opponent checked himself, but before he looked back up, Fabian had landed a right hand on the cranium. A shot I was going to become familiar with in the future. A shot that hits the soft part of your skull vibrating your brain and shutting the light out quickly—a knockout shot.

My philosophy meant that I should encourage this kind of behaviour, championing the cause by standing up on my chair and shouting into the cage something equally aggressive. I could have easily come up with a better insult than "Melon".

A blonde lady wearing a push-up bra and much make-up began flirting with Greeny at the end of the row.

I noticed this girl do laps of the arena, looking for horny men. I saw her find them, and I even noticed her receive cash.

She was almost definitely a prostitute.

Greeny started fumbling through his wallet, looking for cash.

Soll and I watched in our peripheral, thinking, "Here, surely not."

"We take card, babe," she said whilst pulling out a small portable card machine. The look on Greeny, James, Soll, mine and two other random geezers said it all. We were flabbergasted; I mean, first Joe & The Juice and now hookers.

I thought we had more time.

"Do you take Amex?" Greeny asked.

"Yeah, sugar."

They take Amex too.

"THAT'S FUCKING BRILLIANT," I said, pointing to the machine.

"What's next, Coutts?" James replied.

"We take that too," she replied.

Some Tescos won't even take Coutts cards. So we were understandably very surprised.

The oldest profession in the world is modernising with the times. Greeny walked out of the arena to the bathrooms with her.

We couldn't help but shout:

"ASK FOR CASHBACK!" Soll shouted.

"TELL HER YOU NEED A RECEIPT FOR SERVICES RENDERED!" James added.

We all sat down once he left. Bored by the fighting, we couldn't see anything, even being a couple of rows back. This sucked; watching fighting is way better from the comfort of your home.

Greeny came out looking sour. Like, I-just-fucked-a-prostitute-at-a-Bellator-fight sour.

Some post-nut-clarity scenarios are clearer than others.

The man pulled out cotton swabs and asked, "Have you answered me correctly thus far?"

"Yes. Are you sure you want me to keep talking?" I asked, genuinely concerned. He flicked through the medical record and looked back up at me.

"Well, it's making sense of a lot of the blood work and hospital visits that you've had this year."

"Great, well, can we just get the thing done now?"

"This is illegal, Courtney; we have to go through the appropriate checks."

"Where is the nurse? I've got places to be."

"What places?"

I paused. "I don't know—Vegas, mate. Anywhere, just not here on a Friday, no offence."

"None taken."

"So you were:

"ON THE WAY TO THE SQUARE"

We all calmed down and got composed. I say we calmed down, but in reality, we just did a bunch of ketamine in the back of the cab.

There were some rules to going to clubs such as The Square that one must always follow.

Rule one: Spend a lot of money; luckily for me, we had two people in the group capable of doing so.

Rule two: If you are kicked out of the club, remind said club promoters that you spent a lot of money.

Rule three: If you don't have any money, pretend you have a lot of money. Alternatively, go a lot with people who do have a lot of money. Guilty by association.

Rule four: Spend a lot of money on good cologne. It's not paramount, but I've heard through the grapevine that models can smell cheap cologne from a mile away.

We arrived, and Soll smugly walked to the front of the line past a row of wealthy bankers, attractive influencers and snotty-nosed European rich kids.

We swaggered with him, dressed like we were going to be in the papers. We held a united front of confidence.

We are not The Square's typical miscreants. So, suspicion from bouncers was to be expected.

"I'd like to speak with Sara?" Soll said to a bouncer twice his size in height and thrice in width.

The bouncer looked at us sceptically. We were irregular regulars at the club.

I could tell that he could vaguely remember our faces but wasn't willing to let us in without making sure.

Soll had that entitled-to look on his face; you'll know the one; it's a face that says: "I have never gone through any hardship thus far. I probably won't in future. Oh, and also, my house has two Agas, and I have enough money in my ISA to buy a large boat."

"What's your name?" the bouncer asked.

"Solomon."

The bouncer turned and checked a list. "No Solomon on the list."

It got awkward, and our faces dropped. James took two precautionary steps back from the group just in case we weren't allowed in.

"You need to go to the back of the queue," the bouncer said just loud enough so that everyone in the queue could hear.

"I HAVE BOOKED A TABLE." Soll's ego spiralled in front of our very own eyes.

"Look, can you get Sara to come out? She knows us," I said a little more calmly. He didn't like the look of us. I didn't either, but no one inside the club was exactly an upstanding citizen.

"Just get Sara." Even Greeny was asking now. James pretended to be on the phone.

He loudly announced to nobody:

"Yeah, yeah, if they don't let me in The Square, I'll just have to go to the event they're throwing at the White City House and spend ten thousand pounds on picantes."

An attempt at proving to everyone in the crowd that he had options. I cringed initially and then whispered to him:

"Put me on the guest list." Just in case this didn't work out.

• • • • • • • • • • • •

A couple of minutes of awkward standing, fake conversations and subtle drug use passed.

Sara poked her head out from the great big black door and looked at us. Soll was in front of me but a head shorter. So her eyes met mine.

"Oh, let them in; Courtney spends loads of money here."

I had gone to The Square on many occasions—perhaps in the forties—and I had talked to Sara many times, too. But I had never spent a penny here, not one.

So the notion that she thought I was a big spender upset James and Soll deeply because it was a title they were far more deserving of.

• • • • • • • • • • • •

Soll turned and looked at me spitefully.

"You cheeky fucker."

James laughed as we walked in.

"You slimy cheeky fucker. I love it, it's brilliant," he repeated. "You are such a cheeky fucking bastard."

He repeated in gleeful disbelief.

This was in line with our 2021 philosophy.

Any acts of manipulation, debauchery, fraud, excess or greed should be accompanied by a compliment such as "Brilliant", "Good", or "I love it." As a rule of thumb, always champion unsavoury behaviour.

The club is littered with filthy rich people, all there to watch abhorrent things happen.

There have always been rumours that circulate about The Square.

Such as spiking their drinks or that they fill the air conditioners with Rohypnol particles to make you forget what happened.

You would be an idiot to believe in such things; however, I have blacked out there on many an occasion. Almost two-thirds of all occasions.

To be honest, this is more likely my fault than the fault of anyone else. But the point is that the club is the stuff of legend.

It's situated in the heart of Soho, but you'd never find it; there are no signs, just a line, a bouncer and a big black door.

When you enter, there's a tunnel lit by dark lights that dimly illuminate the misdeeds that go on inside.

The floor has a black flora-covered carpet which reaches all around the club from the door to the smoking area.

It's an Alice in Wonderland kind of place. The place reeks of hedonism. If vampires were real, they were probably here.

You walk up through the dark tunnel into a vibrant main floor. The main floor is illuminated exclusively by a couple of circulating spotlights. When you're in the spotlight, everyone in the club can see you; when you're not, you can do whatever you want. To the right, you can see a massive stage. Atop that stage, naked transvestites, dwarfs, cabaret dancers, and sometimes even lucky guests receive sexual favours.

To the left of the stage is a giant dancing platform raised a metre off the ground; it's the most illuminated part of the club, and there are usually five high-end disguised prostitutes dancing atop it.

Two staircases wrap around the platform and lead to a large intimidating bar twelve metres high and as wide as the room. You can get anything your heart desires as long as the cash in your pocket can supply it.

On each staircase, there are five tables along the stairs; these tables are separated from the main floor by a small white Georgian-style bannister and four security guards wearing tuxedos.

The more you pay, the higher your table is up, starting anywhere from five thousand pounds to fifteen.

James and Soll chose the average at ten.

We were led in by a naked lady, who took our jackets and led us to our table. An amalgamation of ketamine made the blurry figures in the room indistinguishable. I squinted with one eye and held the Georgian bannister, looking out and around the club. Faces and blurs passed me by, faint laughs, darting stares, and frantic movement surrounded me. I was stuck in the rapids, surrounded by moving people but not able to move.

I clutched the bannister, noticing the bouncers' attention was starting to zone in on me. I just had to get to the safety of the table, and then I'd recompose myself.

The bouncers watched as I pulled myself up the stairs using the bannister to pass table after table. I finally reached the table and waited for my senses to return.

Paranoia kicked in, and everyone in the vicinity was talking about me.

My friends, the girls, and the bouncers. I couldn't hear what they were saying, but I knew that it was along the lines of "He needs to go."

A bouncer on the other side of the club whispered and pointed at me. I tried to duck behind an unsuspecting table girl, but I tripped and fell back to my seat instead. I had to recompose myself, or I would be removed. The shadows could only protect me for so long.

Soll looked at me slumped on the leather sofa and slid his finger under his nose or his neck, then pointed at me. The only reason I even knew it was Soll was because of his Jewfro.

He either wanted me to die, or he wanted me to use the great leveller.

I poured some cocaine out onto the table when the bouncer

wasn't looking, flopped onto the floor beside it, angled my neck at a ninety-degree angle and sniffed it all, rubbing my nose against the cold glass.

I lay staring up at the ceiling next to the table and waited for it to kick in. I spat on my hand and wiped my face and nose of any evidence.

I took a couple of breaths and hit my vape, praying for some nicotine energy. Breathe in... hold... breathe out.

"I'M FUCKING BACK," I jumped up and shouted.

The bouncers averted their attention to someone else in the club.

Being high on cocaine in an expensive club in London is essentially as socially acceptable as drinking a pint of cider in a pub. People will notice and talk, but no one is gonna bring you up on it.

A couple of bottles of Grey Goose vodka caught the eyes of some table girls in limbo.

There is kind of an unspoken rule with table girls that in exchange for drinks, they will gently stroke your ego.

"What do you guys do?" a pretty blonde shouted in mine and Greeny's ear. Without hesitation, both of us said: "Crypto."

Shameful, but copywriter and aspiring DJ weren't gonna fly here. Greeny asked her:

"And what do you do, darling?"

Without hesitation, she replied, "OnlyFans."

We looked her up and down and decided that it checked out.

She then started to blather on about how OnlyFans was a good way to make money.

"You know what we both have in common?" I asked her rhetorically. "Both our professions are bullshit," I answered.

I mean mine because I was lying and hers because, well, she sells naked videos of herself.

I wasn't judging her, though; she wanted a good life, a smooth cruise, her way, and she felt she was entitled to it. I couldn't judge her; I felt it, too.

She was upset that I called her profession bullshit. I mean, who was I to judge? I tried to defuse the situation.

"The point is neither of us is a doctor."

"I fucked a doctor once," she replied.

"Well, that's the same thing as being one," I replied sarcastically.

"WHAT!" she shouted back.

After a bit more shouting, I noticed neither of us was really communicating.

We just shouted and nodded along, unaware of what the other person was saying. This nodding and shouting ritual went on for about ten minutes until I gave up trying to communicate, and we just kissed and then went to the bathroom to have sex.

I came back to the table after, I want to say, twenty minutes, but it was probably more like two, and started dancing again.

The girl I had just slept with's friend was now trying to compete with her and started to kiss me, too. I did not mind being their object to play with.

However.

She tasted like truffle oil, so I sat down and ignored them. I don't like truffles.

I stayed seated until the show started.

I was heavily inebriated by this point, so I won't bore you with specifics. Essentially a transvestite with massive tits and a massive cock shat on a naked female dwarf and then proceeded to get blown by said dwarf until completion. Proper, wholesome stuff.

The truffle oil chick started pestering me with questions, and I was too inebriated to answer. Eventually, she got the message after I started to sway, so she went to talk to James instead.

She wouldn't find much luck over there; his jaw was bouncing off the ceiling.

I looked around the club, sedated and nostalgic, reminiscing on the first time I was here five years ago.

I had thirty pounds on my debit card, and I was talking to a stunning French lady who was twice my age.

Somehow, I was wearing a red Adidas tracksuit. Well, I say somehow.

But in actuality, Soll and I had snuck in through the smoking area.

Anyway, I asked this lady with the hubris of youth:

"Are you alone tonight, madam?"

That is a lie; I probably said something more to the effect of:

"WhAt yoo say'in, MaDaM, cAn I gEt YoU a DrInK?" in a drunken Jack Sparrow-esque stupor.

This stupor was acquired by downing a Lucozade Glens mix minutes prior. I wouldn't touch the stuff now.

She obliged regardless, and I ordered two gin and tonics, pulled out my orange under-eighteens NatWest card that had never seen north of five hundred pounds and tapped confidently.

Declined.

I tapped again, knowing the inevitable outcome. Declined again.

The bartender knew I had no money just from how I was dressed. I looked at the lady like a little boy who had been caught red-handed stealing; my only defence mechanism was innocence, so I smiled awkwardly.

To her displeasure, she ended up buying both drinks for fifty pounds and scurried off, embarrassed that she had even talked to me. A hilarious twist of fate.

However, I stole a drink from the smoking area that was spiked that night and ended up falling over a bannister onto a group of old rock stars and supermodels. Almost as though God planned it, Soll also threw up directly over two models that night around four seconds later.

Needless to say, we were promptly removed by two angry security guards and banned for life.

That ban was removed one year later when Soll and I used fake IDs to get in, and he spent seven thousand pounds on vodka alone.

That money he actually had acquired from Bitcoin. It was up at that point. Good times.

After doing some more coke with Greeny, I stood up energised, and we got chatting with the girls at the table.

One of them asked, "Do you want a private show?"

Soll pushed me out of the way and handed her his Amex. "GIVE US THE MOST EXPENSIVE ONE YOU'VE GOT!"

"Follow me."

Greeny, Soll and I went downstairs whilst James chatted to the girl with truffle breath and could have been a hooker.

On the lower level, there are booths with private bars. The walls are lined with fractured mirrors, distorting our reflections appropriately sinisterly.

We sat in a booth and ordered three negronis.

We sat in a booth and waited for a private show which involved a girl using her anus to paint on his back and writing "Happy Birthday" in it.

It wasn't his birthday.

But I thought it was funny, so I told her it was.

James entered the room halfway through the painting and brought with him some rather negative energy.

James, the entitled toff that he was so capable of being, tried against all of our wills to kiss this anus-paint lady.

The girl appropriately slapped him as hard as possible, the paintbrush still firmly placed in her butt.

Within an instant, a security guard came in, grabbed him by the neck and pulled him out.

We could faintly hear him shout arrogantly and snarkily outside the booth: "You can't remove me from here, I'm the king, UNHAND ME, RHINOCEROS!" James was unaware of his surroundings at this point, both metaphorically and literally.

His snarky shouts didn't stop, but they did get harder to hear the further he was removed from the club.

James was charged an extra three thousand pounds for the

girl's troubles and for calling the bouncer a "Rhinoceros".

Once James left, I stayed an extra minute with Greeny, my face bright red from laughing. I asked her if she was all right, and she said:

"You should all be put on a leash."

This comment didn't get to me, but I saw in Soll's face he had had a realisation. He got up and went to the bathroom; I followed to make sure he was okay.

The broken mirror bounced our reflections around the floor, distorting our vision and making it very hard to find the bathroom.

He was distraught when I found him in the bathroom. The early onset of frantic self-doubt that would probably riddle his Sunday slowly started to crack through his bravado.

He was wired, pacing back and forth in a marble toilet cubicle. He asked me, "Do you have any ketamine?" I didn't.

"I NEED TO GET OUT OF HERE!"

I thought about it.

We needed to pay and look presentable to get out of this predicament.

It's hard to look presentable when you have a stripper's butt painting on your back. To make matters worse, she must have used permanent ink because I had to peel the words "Happy Birthday" off his back. There's some irony somewhere in that.

Secondly, Soll was inebriated to the point where he had lost all of his possessions, including his wallet, phone and even his shirt.

This meant he could not pay. This was a troublesome ordeal, as this wasn't the kind of joint where you could scrub the dishes for a night to pay what you owed. I stuck my head out of the bathroom door; it appeared that two security guards had followed us to the bathroom as a friendly reminder that we owed the club money.

"Um, so how much do we owe?" I asked, thinking about how much money I had in my overdraft.

"Twenty-five thousand."

We owed twenty-five thousand pounds, which was not good because my overdraft maxed out at two thousand, and Soll only had Apple Pay.

"Right, we'll be out in just a second."

I thought hard about this.

The thought crossed my mind that Soll could perform some kind of sexual favour to an old rich guy.

But after deep thought, I concluded that Soll would be rather upset if I made him do such a thing.

Think, Courtney, think.

I had a faulty Amex I had found on the floor at Entrecôte a week prior. That's it. I'd go with the guards whilst Soll escaped through the smoking area; I'd give them the faulty card. Pretend to go to the bathroom and run out of the smoking area.

I slapped Soll four times and then dunked his head in cold water until he became alert.

"We need to fucking go," I said, holding the Amex. He looked up at it.

"It's a gold card; they'll never believe you," he said dramatically whilst leaning over the sink, almost in tears.

"SHUT UP, DON'T SAY THINGS LIKE THAT! They'll have to believe me."

I slapped him again. Then took off my jacket and gave it to him so he wouldn't be shirtless.

"I'm going to give them this card; you need to escape through the smoking area whilst I do this. DO YOU UNDERSTAND ME?"

He nodded.

I walked out and went with the security guards to the front.

I handed the manager the faulty Amex card and casually told her I needed to go to the bathroom. By the time she had turned around, I had already slinked out into the shadows of the Soho streets.

There are plenty more clubs in London anyway.

I left the club holding up Soll, who was now shirtless, covered in sick and still heavily sedated. We limped toward some steps around the corner from the club, and I ordered a Bolt. Because Bolt is cheaper, and ordering an Uber in Soho takes forty minutes.

I pulled out a cigarette, and we shared it. Well, I say we shared it, but I had one pull, and then Soll slobbered the end with sick, so I let him finish it.

"Hey," a pleasant voice said from the right of me.

I lifted an eyebrow and squinted suspiciously until the figure emitting the sound came into focus.

I couldn't believe it; the tides had shifted. An angel had arrived.

Soll threw up onto himself with impeccably bad timing. Déjà vu.

"Ew, gross!"

I quickly surveyed the situation and appropriately decided to change the topic: "How's your Friday going? I think I saw you at that New Year's post-COVID-19 party thing."

I felt like the best way to handle this scenario was to ignore Soll's presence completely.

"It's a Saturday, and I think I saw you staring," she said, disappointed.

"Oh, it is Saturday. I wasn't staring; I was surveying so that I could build up the courage to ask you out."

She paused and sniffed me, took a step back. "Go on then."

My cologne had worked.

"Do you want to go out?" I pleaded and held my phone out for her to use.

"Maybe."

Despite her remark, she took my phone and put in her details.

"Is your friend going to be all right?" she said, pointing at Soll, who was murmuring something inaudible in the background.

To my dismay and surprise, without my supervision, he had gotten up, managed to waddle back to the corner of the club and piss on the side of it.

The bouncers didn't mind, which makes me think that the gold Amex I left them with was charged. Some git is going to wake up with minus twenty-five thousand.

The thought humoured me.

By the time I had fully grasped the situation, she had put my phone back into my hand and walked off. I looked down at her profile; she was tangible, and her name was Amora, or more precisely, her Instagram name @AmorAmorMore.

Rarely has a man attracted women on scent alone; rarer still has a man attracted a woman without.

"Courtney, why do you want this now?"

"Like I said, I've got places to be… everyone says you're the guy who can get this done early and legally so that it's on the system."

"You do know there will be side effects."

"Do you think, after everything I've told you, that I am the kind of guy to care about side effects?"

He shook his head, poured the ethanol into a small cup, and placed a cotton bud next to it.

"She's almost here; carry on telling your story."

"Well, I was infatuated with this girl from the first time I saw her, so I went…"

CHAPTER 7

"WHEN I WOKE UP"

I was at Soll's house naked next to a girl snoring. I prayed and prayed in my mind that it was Amora; I quietly peered over at her and looked. It was not, which meant I needed to message her. I rolled out of bed and walked through Soll's house in Hampstead. To get to the toilet, I had to walk through the main hall where Soll's dad was reading a paper. He was used to this kind of next-day 3 p.m. hungover stupidity and just shouted, "CLOTHES!"

I noticed I was walking around the house naked. I nodded and then ran to the shower and sat on the toilet, trying to think of the perfect line of copy to get Amora on a date. It needed to be witty and concise to get this girl's attention and offset any drunken Jack Sparrow damage I may have caused last night. Well, I mean this morning.

The thing about the perfect DM (direct message on Instagram) is that it needs to directly encapsulate what your aim is in as few words as possible. There are, of course, rules you have to play by when in the DMs. Firstly, do not give the opposite sex too much attention, which I had broken already. Secondly, be direct, which I had also not been very good at last night, and thirdly, get them off of their device and at a bar as quickly as possible. There is a nuance to this; when online, the opposite gender holds all the power, they just do. Men generally act like dogs, and we are essentially excited by the slightest advances by women. Women are a lot smarter and picky. So, I had to create the perfect amount of charm, self-deprecation, gentlemanliness and mystery if I was to have a shot at gaining her attention.

You do not want to come on too strong with a crappy pickup line. However, those do work in the right context. So after attempt number three hundred: "Embarrassed about yesterday, but I did get your details, so can I make it up to you by buying you a lot of drinks this Wednesday?" Well, it's not gonna win a Booker Award, but it was going to have to do. I broke it down.

Admit fault: check.

Give clear prerogative: check.

Insinuating potential alcoholism: check.

Now sit staring at your phone for five hours in anticipation, endlessly doom-scrolling your anxiety until:

Voila, she replies, "Yeah, I'd love to." Now I have to wait another five hours to reply, to show that I'm not as eager as I am.

Five hours later: "You choose the spot; I'll choose the time."

I always let the girl choose the bar to meet at because then the ball is in their court. They have to impress you with their choice. Time rarely varies. She chose a small jazz bar in Soho.

The bar was squished between two money-laundering fronts, a fortune teller and a Thai massage parlour. The outside had no windows and a sign that said "Jaz's Jazz". The second "Jazz" was crooked. When you enter the bar, it's cramped, and the ceiling is low. If you're above six feet, you have to bend down low. The walls are covered with naked Page 3 girls from the noughties, which are held up by masking tape and pins. There is a large light-up Father Christmas next to the stage covered in fairy lights, which is the only actual light in the room.

The bar is not impressive or comfortable. It only serves one purpose: jazz.

Nothing about the bar screamed, "Look at me," or "Please come in here." No, it's anti-TikTokers, socialites and floppy-haired emo types that seem to be coming into fashion these days; this bar said, "You are not welcome."

It was dark inside; the owner was old school and led me to the table by pointing to it with a cigarette. The regulars looked at me as I strolled in.

The only guy in the bar alone, the only guy in the bar below forty-five years of age, the only guy who didn't have a drink and a suit to match.

But it didn't matter; I wanted that, and I would rather feel like an outsider in this place than an insider at "Be At One".

The thought of Be At One made me a little sick.

I sat down; the waiter asked me what I wanted to drink. This was the precipice before the precipice.

"Whiskey, rocks, lots of rocks."

She eyed me up, and the room went quiet.

"What whiskey? Jack? Jameson? Or Southern Comfort?"

She's testing me; the trick question—Southern Comfort is bourbon, and Jack, well, Jack is whack.

This wasn't the type of place where they had expensive drinks; no, this was the kind of place where they had good drinks, and knowing the difference was paramount.

"Jameson, rocks, lots of rocks."

She nodded, the jazz players relaxed back into their chairs, the music continued, and I became a part of the decor.

I looked at my surroundings; it was small, it was cramped, the drinks were cheap, the music was live, and not a single pair of skinny jeans or veneers was in the vicinity. The kind of people who knew about this bar knew jazz, and they lived it. Our seat was in the far left back corner, about eight metres away from the band.

Tucked away, out of sight, just how I liked.

Amora walked in; she was insanely attractive, and she knew exactly what most other men and I seek. Two things: the prospect of sex and the subsequent denial of it. When done right, the glorious toxic harmony comes into play, and what you can't have, you want more. She played me at my own game; she turned up twenty minutes later than the time we agreed, which meant I had consumed four double Jamesons on the rocks, which was not a healthy amount to be saying hello to anyone, let alone a girl with such a large and quantifiably self-endowed psychological advantage over me.

She walked into the bar; she wasn't overdressed; she had hit the mark perfectly between sexy and casual. She had a little bit of black eyeliner with pink highlighter on her eyelids, her hair was in a bun, which showed me her perfect profile, and her lips were dark red, almost indica. She wore two big gold hoops and a diamond necklace with the word "Love" spelt backwards, spelling "Evol", resting above her cleavage.

She was in an expensive but tattered-looking slinky crop top that had a button at the bottom undone. Baggy mum jeans. Blue retro Jordan fours and acrylic nails that spelt out something bitchy.

She hugged me, sat up straight on the chair in front of me, stared into the depths of my soul, smiled whilst maintaining eye contact and said, "Get me a drink then."

I thought of all the possible cool and collected ways I could reply, but I just smiled, pulled out my card, handed it to the bartender, and told him to get her however many anythings she wanted.

All the while holding her eye contact back, she had the keys, she was in the driver's seat, her hand was on the wheel, and her foot was pressed on the accelerator; she wasn't looking at me. She was looking ahead at the road. She wanted to see if my bravado was a bluff.

I asked her:

"Why this place?"

Saying it, though, I was unimpressed. She showed her hand. "Jazz is real."

"As opposed to?" I asked, raising her.

She shrugged, reached over and sipped my drink.

"What do you do?" I asked.

She said, "You don't care," with nonchalant confidence.

"How do you know that I don't care?" I didn't care.

"You don't care because I don't care."

"Right, well, let's not care together then."

All the while, she stared at me, never breaking eye contact, except occasionally and appropriately to look at the naked ladies on the wall or the jazz.

So we sat and listened to jazz, not caring about one another, until she got up and sat next to me. She effortlessly moved around the table as though the space was hers. She was aware of her effect. It was fascinating, so I just watched her like a man seeing a tiger for the first time. I knew it existed, but I never thought I would see one up close. She watched the jazz and gave me the signals that she wanted me to make a move. The classic roll of the hair above the ear. So I leaned my head in next to her ear and said softly, plainly and most importantly, directly:

"I care a little bit more now."

She smiled and turned her head. She looked up toward me, puppy-eyed. I could feel her breath enter my nose, and I got that feeling, a warm feeling, natural, safe; if it could speak, her breathing said, "It's all right, you're going to be okay." Our lips collided, and it felt like it was already over even though it had just begun; everything up till this point led me to her; she was the answer to this feeling of boredom, a sense of purpose, someone I could create stories with. We spent the rest of the night kissing aggressively at the back of the club until it closed.

On the way to getting my thirteenth drink of the night, I caught a glimpse of myself in the mirror; I looked lean, with just the right amount of stubble, hair perfectly giving the illusion that no time was put into it. If it could speak, it would say: "I make it look easy."

It was time to call it a night; she wasn't going to come back with me; she was too smart for that. Regardless, I didn't want that for her; she deserved more. So, as the last song played and the music filled the room, I whispered, "I'm going to head home." I can't remember if it was a shout or a whisper, but she nodded, kissed me on the cheek and swaggered out underneath the dark fluorescent purple "Jaz's Jazz" sign and walked away.

As I walked back home, I felt the endorphins of love. Excitement and happiness rolled over me like waves; even the whiskey that sloshed around my vetted stomach could not break my mood. I skipped down the dark, packed Soho roads giddily.

The shadows loomed over me, chasing my glow, trying to bring me back. Everywhere I looked, the commercial bars, the casinos and the massage parlours were packed with young men and women. I ignored them, walking toward Leicester Square station.

On the way, I noticed a large group of young men entering the Windmill strip club, hypnotised by the allure of sex, flashing lights and thumping music. On the other side of the road, young girls waited in queues before club bouncers who weighed up whether or not their God-given attributes were good enough to be worthy of getting in. Brilliant.

The neon signs pull at your desires; you can feel it, your soul pulls away, you wrestle with it, and your spirit floats above you, tugging at your shoulders to turn around, go home, watch fucking *Bridgerton* and do some good work tomorrow. You might listen, or you might lose.

After a series of twists and turns through a small dark, and dingy passage, I approach an old French pub near Leicester Square station—you know, the one that's been around since before the First World War. As I look across the road, three figures emerge from a black Mercedes. It's Soll, James, and Greeny. They're just far enough away that I could slip past and go home, leave untainted, eat some spaghetti, and read *Why the Scandinavians Do It Better*. "Looks good," the whiskey says.

Soll runs past on the other side of the road, and a sense of relief fills me up. I turn and watch him frolic into the darkness of Soho, arms sprawled out like an aeroplane, no doubt toward mischief, no doubt aimless, no doubts.

Not tonight, not me; I need to work on a brief tomorrow. But wait, what if the girl of my dreams is in there? What if this is the night where all the boys meet Leonardo DiCaprio, and we find out that Anthony Bourdain isn't dead, he's just been hiding with Tupac on that island, and tonight is the night that they'll be at a club, and maybe they'll tell me some stories. I convince myself that I would rather live in that fantasy than live in the reality that I'm going to sit at a desk and talk to Naomi for nine hours about how we can optimise our Hinge profiles to get more matches tomorrow.

So I shout, "WHAT ARE YOU CUNTS DOING HERE!" as I run up to them. Greeny stops swaying drunkenly, spins around, and runs like a gorilla toward me—you know, the one that Conor McGregor patented; he struts to within an inch of my face, like a stare-off before a fight and says with pissy-smelling Stella beer breath:

"We like to drink with Courtney 'cause Courtney is our mate, we like to drink with Courtney 'cause he's one of our mates, we like to drink with Courtney, and it's not up for debate!" Brilliant.

And so we did; we drank down the streets of Soho, pissing down alleyways, flicking cigarettes in the direction of bouncers and shouting obscenities at one another to the point of abuse.

Chasing something we could never catch.

"Where are we going?" I ask, being the only one in the group relatively sober.

"Elizabeth's," James said, trying to hide the pride in his voice.

"That'll do."

"Know when to call it."

The man smiled; I could tell he liked that story.

"I like that one; it reminds me of when I was young." Next to the ethanol and swabs, he placed a large needle.

I looked down at the floor, sick from the sight of it. "Why is this taking so long?"

"This was very hard to get, Courtney; it's imported straight from Egypt; keep speaking. The nurse will be here any moment now."

"All right, fine; I went to Elizabeth's in Mayfair with James, Greeny and Soll.

CHAPTER 8

THE UBER PULLS UP OUTSIDE ELIZABETH'S, AND UPON EXIT

Paparazzi swarm Greeny as the event's host personally greets him and James. Most of them shout, "WHERE'S YOUR MUM!" to James and "LOOK HERE" to Greeny. Both Greeny and James are trying tremendously hard not to look pleased with themselves.

Between the blaring flashes, the paparazzi's faces seem unsure of whom they are photographing.

Soll and I kick the dirt in the background like two extras on a movie set. We talk to one another about meaningless drivel to appear like we are not lost tourists.

"Have you seen the state of the economy?" I say, noticing that this is the first time in my life that those words have ever come out of my mouth.

"Yes, quite disappointing; it appears we are going into a bull market; even the Saudis are worried."

I know Soll knows absolutely nothing about the economy, and yet I still feel inclined to believe every word he's saying; perhaps I'm stereotyping his Jewishness.

James and Greeny enter, and we follow with blind arrogance and confidence. Once again, looking at all the chumps in the line begging to get in, we weren't like them; they were losers, and we didn't wait in lines or dress up for these sorts of things.

So naturally, Soll stuck his tongue out at the three city boys at the front of the line.

The door lady kissed James and Greeny on the cheek each and welcomed them in, telling the bouncer, "No need to ID or search them, and make sure you give this one lots of free drinks once he's inside."

She fake-smiled at James.

Once he looked away, she mouthed to her assistant, "His mum is the host." I love it.

Soll and I walked behind them expecting the same treatment but were rudely stopped in our complacent tracks.

"And who are you two?"

We both look ahead into the dark passage that leads to the club; the thumping music just reaches our ears and lets us know what we are going to miss if we don't get in.

I take a step back, and Soll follows; we have reached an impasse. Greeny and James have no intention of helping us get in, not now, not whilst their egos are being stroked inside.

We were on our own.

The heroes were to face off against the gatekeeper and the troll; if we couldn't pass this level, surely we would be no match for the bosses inside.

Soll used his special move, fake name-dropping:

"I am Soll Bartholomew Jones the Tenth, and this is Courtney of the Courts of Cartwright."

"Not on the list," the lady snapped back, chewing gum and unaffected by Soll's advance.

"Allow me." I pushed in front of Soll to have a crack at the moody door lady myself.

"Is Christian inside? We are on his list, and if Christian doesn't come up, then try Kristina." I use a flamboyant wave upwards whilst saying both names to add dramatic effect.

"No Christian or Kristina on the list." This was a lie; there is always at least one of those at a party like this.

It was personal now.

Soll stood back and looked outward from the rope barrier to disassociate himself from me on the off chance that either Greeny or James decided to turn back and help him get in.

There was no hope, no future; we were to walk the plank with the people we had so quickly labelled losers, now our comrades.

The bouncer directed us with one large muscular finger to walk to the back of the queue, further back than the group of bankers we had so eagerly stuck out our tongues at, and of course, they returned the favour as we headed beyond them.

We took it on the chin, the games, the game.

As we walked further to the back of the line, the crowd went from bad to worse. At the front, it's rich bankers, rich kids, hot girls and models.

Being compared to them is not so bad; I could live with that.

But at the back, it was aspiring influencers and stragglers. The hypocrisy of it all—we were surrounded by us's. It was terrifying. They all shared the same look, a look that screamed, "I'll be inside in no time."

I felt sick; even though none of them were in fancy dress, they all thought with such blind arrogance that there was no way they couldn't be let in despite not being invited.

Was this who we were? Were we so egotistical to think that we were individuals, different, special even?

We held our heads in shame, listening to the oh-so-familiar conversations going on around us.

"Mike is inside; he will have put me on the list."

"Gemma, I'm outside; I thought Kate Moss's assistant said you had two plus ones."

I vomited in my mouth, but just before all hope was lost, a glimmer of hope seemed to be headed our way; James's mother walked down the line with the door lady and pointed at us.

Aha, we were different after all. The ogre unhooked the rope, and we were escorted in, knights returning valiantly from battle; the castle was ours, untouchable, ready to enjoy the spoils of war once inside.

Elizabeth's looks like a gingerbread house, except instead of the usual things you get in a gingerbread house, like gingerbread, chocolate and candy, you have gold leaf, ivory and pink gems.

It's a fairyland with golden pillars and arches, green rooms with plants, and a bar that glows green with emeralds reflecting chequered floor tiles. Every room is a different present, every room a new opportunity.

A wonderland.

As you look from one end to the other, every single person looks as though they have been given a handwritten invitation from the creative director of the magazine hosting the event themselves; the place reeks of smugness and main character syndrome. People dressed in tailored suits and designer dresses, everyone trying their absolute hardest to appear as though they belong.

Soll and I collect two gin and tonics from a suspicious barman, and we turn and look out to target where the source of the fun is coming from.

"Shall we begin?" I say to Soll, smiling at an older lady walking by.

"I think we shall."

"You see a target yet?" Soll sips.

"Yep, two models over there, jaws bouncing."

"So what should we be tonight?" Soll says, looking forward at the crowd and sipping his now second gin and tonic.

I let the statement breathe for a couple of minutes.

"I'm thinking models."

"Okay, let's do models."

We both get into character; I pout a little, not too much, just enough to look like I take myself very seriously, just enough to believe modelling is a career worth having a conversation over. Soll runs his fingers through his perm-like hair, and we both cock our shoulders for better posture. I unbutton my shirt to reveal my chest.

"What are you doing?" Soll remarks, looking at my chest. I do my shirt back up.

"Shall we?"

"We shall."

We make a direct beeline to two tall, thin African models with perfectly symmetrical faces in head-to-toe leather and fluorescent green sunglasses. They're holding unlit cigarettes and standing by the door high as fuck.

"Hi, I'm Courtney, and this is my friend Soll. Do you have a spare cigarette by any chance?" I pout a little, and Soll tenses his non-existent jaw.

They look us up and down to assess whether we are worth their time.

"Of course you can, honey." One of them pulls out a menthol Vogue cigarette; I cringe internally at the thought of having to smoke it but bear with it.

"So what do you guys do?" Soll asks, knowing the answer.

"I'm a model, babe," the slightly taller one said, offended that we had to ask.

"Us too, us too," I respond; a very awkward silence fills the room as they look at us with hesitation; one of them even raises an eyebrow in disbelief.

"Baby Gap," the other one chimes in, revealing she's French.

Soll and I are now offended and, sure, a little bitter; I am aware that gunning for models may come from a place of insecurity, but look, sometimes pretty people need to be put in their place.

"So, did you guys always want to be models, or were you born without ambition?" I say just loud enough for Soll to hear and just quiet enough for them to second-guess what I said.

They squint at me, like, did "he just say that to our faces?" I carry on like I said nothing out of the ordinary; they arrogantly bite the bait and answer as though my question were not an insult.

"I fell into it; I love it, though; it's the lifestyle, the hotels, the money, the parties, the runway, the glitz and the glamour."

"Me too," Soll replies, then continues:

"Personally, when teachers asked me what I wanted to be when I was older, I used to look them dead in the eye and say, 'I want to get changed for a living, you know, put on some clothes, take them off, put them back on; that's the kind of thing that just really, you know, it inspired me; I wanted to add nothing to society and get paid for it.'"

The models nod as though we had said something very profound that they related to on a spiritual level.

We are perplexed but decide that this is as good a time as any to exit. We laugh, thank them for the cigarette and move on.

Across the bar, I can see James's mum holding court near the bar.

She is viciously confident, an ambitious woman, a man-eater, stoic, terrifying and despises both Soll and me.

Her eyes lock on me, robotic; she zooms in. She ushers me over with a wave. I know this conversation will be unpleasant because she thinks anyone not in fashion is completely irrelevant.

"Hello, Courtney," she says, ignoring Soll completely and purposefully.

"Um, hi, Poppy." She stares at me and forces an awkward silence.

"Great night," I remark, sipping my drink, trying my best to make this not terrible.

"Do you know why I let James bring you to these things?" I knew she was going to say something horrible, so I took it upon myself to start having fun.

"Because I'm so good-looking?" I fake-smiled at her.

She nor her little camp friend found my joke funny. I laughed regardless.

"No, because he is leaving to study in New York in three months at NYU, and the more time he's around you, the more he will understand that mediocrity is not an option." I tilt my head.

Did this bitchy giraffe in all black say that to my face?

"Oh, Poppy, am I so mediocre?" I ask her inquisitively.

"No, darling, of course not, but in all honesty, what are you going to do once my little James and the little man over there leave, too?" She looks over Soll's way; he looks down.

"You're leaving?" I say, a little crushed, in Soll's direction.

"Found out today, mate; I gotta get out of London; it's not healthy," he replied awkwardly.

I couldn't blame him; I would too; New York is like London on steroids—well, to be more specific, Manhattan is like London on steroids—hotter girls, higher-paying jobs, more rich kids to connect with, the Big Apple, the centre of the universe. I wasn't upset because it was ending; I was upset because it was carrying on without me.

She laughs at my sultry face because she got exactly what she wanted; even though music thumped away, there was somehow a silence filling the space between the four of us. Her little underling smiled by her side, so happy that she had taken her anger out on me instead of him for once. What a sad existence.

It dawned on me that I could say whatever I wanted to her; I wasn't going to see James again once he left, so why let her have the last laugh?

So I did.

Before I tell you what I said, I have to explain why it is not allowed; in the superficial world of fashion, there is one thing that you can never say. Fashion is and will always be about being young. So naturally, everyone in the industry lies about their age, especially the older female designers, models, event hosts and creatives, because they're appropriately scared of being replaced by younger, fresher talent.

To give you context, a normal sixty-year-old is a fashion forty.

"Well, luckily for us, James has told me that your sixtieth birthday is coming up soon; I'll see Soll and you there. I'll bring the mediocre gift of my presence as a present. In fact, I know a great health retreat that can help with your jowl," I said, circling her chin.

"And they can help with your crow's feet, too." I circled her eyes, then met them with mine.

Soll winced, and the tiny gay man grimaced.

Her face scrunched up; she wanted to hurt me badly. But in front of all these guests, she had to keep her composure.

This was surely the last one of these parties I would ever get to abuse as a plus one. I took a moment in, and I had signed the contract: no more shitty influencer, fashion or music parties for me. How would I live?

She smiled defiantly, gaining her composure as though my comment were fair game in this instance, but I knew she wouldn't take such a public display of defiance from someone she held in such low regard lightly. Somewhere, somehow in the future, she was going to fuck me; it was only a matter of time.

"Go for the jowl."

Once James got done doing the rounds entertaining his mother's friends, he swaggered over to us with two drinks from the packed bar. Greeny was in the DJ booth pretending to spin decks, and for once, he was killing it; the place was jumping, all the girls were dancing in front of his booth, it was the perfect mix of obscure music from the nineties and equally obscure new rap.

He had hit it on the money; the obscure music meant people felt cool listening to it; it wasn't mainstream, so they didn't feel like they were mainstream either, but it was just well-known enough for every other person in the club to know the lyrics. He was smiling, the girls were losing it, and the guys were buying drinks—a lot of drinks—which made the club owner happy, very, very happy. Sometimes, it's your night; it wasn't mine, but it sure as hell was his. It rarely went this way for him, and I couldn't help but think to myself, live in it, Greeny, live in it now because it won't always be like this.

James got in on our role-play; he pretended to be a shareholder for Elizabeth's to some unsuspecting runway models that fed us coke as though the stuff was on tap; we were completely out of it. The night was a dream; everyone around us blurred into nothingness, and we did our routine gliding from the bar to talk to the older gentlemen about business prospects that we didn't understand with cocaine confidence, then to the stairs to chat to more girls, this time pretending to be married, to see if that would in some way psychologically make them want to kiss us. In fact, at one point, we got so deeply in character that we both found ourselves on two sofas surrounded by five girls, telling them how much we believed in the idea of true love.

My head was in the lap of a cute brunette, and James's head was in a blonde's lap. They stroked our hair, and James would burst out laughing once in a while, temporarily breaking character.

We said things like:

"I love her so much, you know. Have you ever had that love that hurts? That's when I knew I couldn't live without her."

James would rebut my statement, trying to one-up me.

"I thought she would cry when I proposed to her, but I wept; I wept for me; I didn't deserve her."

After about twenty minutes of this, Soll broke after James incorrectly quoted Shakespeare.

"Love looks not with the eyes, but with the mind, and therefore is winged Cupid painted blind."

"You do realise they're lying, right?" Soll said.

James and I looked at Soll and shook our heads subtly; he was going to ruin this perfect scenario. We were getting all our trauma out; sure, we hit them with a white lie about being married, but some of the stuff about love was true.

Modelling is getting changed for a living.

The man looked at me, confused. "What do you do then?"

"Currently unemployed."

The nurse arrived outside the door and said politely, "Sorry for the wait."

Then left to get something outside again.

I kissed my teeth.

Why apologise and then leave again? Makes no sense.

He gestured with a wave and strong eye contact to ignore her and continue.

"Greeny kept saying..."

CHAPTER 9

"OH, WHAT A NIGHT, OH, WHAT A NIGHT."

He jumped up and down, beaming from ear to ear, an excited toddler. A heartwarming sight.

The glory of the perfect night washing over all of us, Soll lay on James's carpet, silent. I could tell something wasn't right.

"I need to fix up, man; we don't have any friends left. Do you remember that before COVID-19, we used to see all kinds of people—people who don't do drugs, people who make music, people with ordinary jobs, and people who went to university?

Where are they? They can't be around us anymore; we've taken it too far, mate."

"But it's a compound year," I said, repeating what Soll had told me once upon a time.

Greeny and James started to rack two lines of Calvin Klein on the table, completely unaffected by Soll's words.

When people tell you that you are the sum of the people you spend the most time with, I always don't believe them because everyone I spend time with is rich, and I'm comparatively broke.

The adventures were going to come to an end; the places I thought I could never go to, the forbidden places, the ones only a select few are allowed to see, and we'd seen them, we'd really seen what they were.

Beyond their shiny exteriors and inner dark decorum, they were just places.

I could see in his eyes that it was over; the spark no longer set ablaze. We were strung out; I was strung out, and I was tired of pretending.

Soll sat back and, in silence, letting the words wash over him, looked out the window; James didn't care. He had already moved to New York in his head. Greeny and I were the last ones left.

I closed my eyes, and I could feel tears, but degenerates don't cry, so I kept them in.

"Oi, James, mate, that's way too—" Soll said abruptly before James inhaled what appeared to be an entire gram of both cocaine and ketamine.

We watched as he stood up.

"I fucking love it," he said, the spark in his eye starting to fade as he waddled backwards.

Soll and I stood to catch him, but before we could, he fell back onto a green lamp, smashing it into loads of pieces.

His eyes rolled back, his body began to shake, and fear crept in. This was it, our reckoning.

I went to grab my phone whilst Greeny held James on his side, trying to scoop the champagne-infused vomit out of his airways with his fingers.

Soll ran downstairs to grab Poppy.

I stood at the top of the stairs watching James convulse, frozen, his vomit spewing out violently onto his mother's Ushak rug.

"POPPY, CALL AN AMBULANCE, CALL AN AMBULANCE!!" Soll yelled downstairs.

Poppy smiled into the crowd of famous actors, rappers, singers and designers, embarrassed, then back at Soll.

"Oh, Solomon, you're always being so funny. Don't worry, folks, he's always like this."

Soll grabbed her arm aggressively and said directly into her ear, "James is overdosing upstairs, and he is going to fucking die." She paused and smiled at her guests.

"Give me a couple of minutes, folks; there's crémant in the fridge if we run out of champagne."

I looked out at the sea of important faces and then back at her. She was completely unfazed; she didn't care.

She directed us up to an empty sitting room with a marble fireplace, took off her white silk gloves and placed them carefully on an expensive glass table.

She took her time, crossed her legs and spoke plainly, emotionlessly and directly. "This has happened before; listen closely because you have about one hour before he dies. If he dies here, my career is over, and you die."

I watched her mouth move, but I couldn't believe what was coming from it; Soll nodded as though this were logical.

"I am going to distract the crowd with a speech in the garden; whilst I do this, Courtney will call an ambulance five doors down."

She took another pause to compose herself.

She pulled out her phone and dialled 999, waited for an answer and then handed me the phone.

"When he is resuscitated, you will get him an Uber to our house in the Cotswolds, and I don't ever want to see either of you again."

I couldn't respond; what could I say? I was so shocked at the information coming out of her mouth.

"NOW GET OUT!"

She shouted, then gritted her teeth like a lion ready to eat both of us.

She composed herself by taking a deep breath, grabbed her silk gloves, put on her fake smile and walked back into the crowd.

Soll and I grabbed him and began to carry him downstairs exactly as she said. His body was convulsing aggressively, and vomit with particles of blood was spraying along the marble floor; Greeny wiped it up with Poppy's mink coat.

That was fitting.

As we carried him down the winding stairs, his eyes were on me, and he was crying; his body was trying its absolute hardest to stay alive, and his eyes were crying; it was the only thing that he had control of—were his tears.

The ambulance came.

They ran out just as she predicted.

He was resuscitated and brought back to life.

Soll, Greeny and I sat on the curb five doors down from the mansion in Kensington.

A car arrived, and we lifted James into it. Soll asked me:

"Are you free in a couple of weeks to say goodbye?"

I nodded.

The car took off with Soll inside.

Greeny got up and began to walk back in the direction of the party.

"Where are you going?" I shouted.

"Back to the party."

I was alone now; I was really and truly alone.

And I had a pitch tomorrow, which made me feel sick because I was going to have to pretend all of this didn't happen.

The show goes on.

"I charge extra for therapy," the dodgy doctor laughed. "Have you ever had a job?"

I think, "Prick."

"Yeah, I had a good one too."

CHAPTER 10

"DO YOU KNOW WHAT IT'S LIKE WORKING A NORMAL JOB?"

I bet you do; it's okay, right? It's nothing amazing; you're not conquering the world or breaking records, but at the end of the day, there are free builders' coffee and Thirsty Thursdays, and week to week, it pays the bills, and occasionally Margaret buys a cake for some guy called John who works in marketing, and there are leftovers so it's not all bad, so you stay, and John's buddy Rachel tells you that if you put your head down and work really, really hard and put your dreams on hold permanently, maybe eventually you can be like her one day and have kids and settle with a guy called Mark, and you and Mark can have date nights and reminisce on when you used to sleep, and one day it'll all be worth it because your kid will grow up and he'll break the cycle.

But they rarely do break the cycle, so you settle for them just having as good a life as you did.

But that doesn't exist anymore.

Unfortunately, Margaret got the last corporate package that you could feasibly buy a house on; John works from home, so there's no birthday cake, the bills are too high to live week to week, and a pink robot calendar will perform Rachel's job in ten years, and date nights will only be in spring and autumn because it'll be too hot to go out in summer and too cold in winter. Having kids is pointless because there won't be enough space for you, let alone you and a baby or teenager. Worse than that, you don't even know what a dream looks like anymore, and most importantly, Thirsty Thursdays aren't even that thirsty; they're slightly eager for a Shandy Thursday with some bloke who talks about the glory days during the eighties, nineties and noughties.

I'm not done. Do you know what it's like having someone assign you a corporate username like:

"@YOURAPERFECTSUNSHINE2021"? Well, let me tell you, it feels a whole lot more like "@YOURNOTGOODENOUGHFOR2021".

Now, I'm no sour patch kid, but these thoughts flood your brain after having five espressos from an artisan coffee truck from a guy who gets his moustache so that each part pokes out.

The weekend drama was clearly getting to me—an overdose there, a friend's mother's unnecessarily cruel comment here, and a friend leaving you behind to go to the land of the free. These are the kinds of things that make going to work on a Monday feel like you're wasting your time.

Monday morning is surely the worst morning of all mornings, enough to make strong men and women weep in cubicles, pray ill upon their superiors and plot hostile takeovers on personal emails.

My usual Mondays were amazing; I woke up twenty minutes before my first meeting, casually slinked out of bed naked, made a French press coffee naked, did one hundred push-ups also naked and played some aggressive drill music with some boxers on because being naked and listening to drill music is one of the most emasculating experiences I am yet to experience.

To give you an example, here is a lyric from my favourite composition:

"IF YOU AIN'T SHOT NOBODY, THEN SHUT UP, SHUT THE FUCK UP!"

After meditating and clearing my head to this wonderful symphony, I would reach down on the floor, pick up a blue polo shirt, put that on and join the Microsoft Teams or Zoom with a big grin. Say quickly, so they know that I'm there: "HELLO, I'M COURTNEY", and then mute my mic and turn my camera off to watch TV until it was time to go out and see my friends or do something I actually enjoyed.

But no, those Mondays were over; we were all called back from our havens and safe places because some dickwad at the top that never comes in anyway decided working in the office was better for the business's productivity and efficiency.

I waddled into the office ten minutes late, soaked by the early November rain, absolutely miserable, disappointed that this was the direction my life seemed to be headed.

I couldn't let them see it, though.

So I shook the rain off, slapped my face whilst staring at the door lady, who was used to this sort of behaviour, recoiled my shoulders, puffed my chest and strutted into the office, head high, smile beaming and flipped them all off internally. I was not a degenerate here; I was a good junior, or that was the perception that I was trying to perpetuate. I walked amongst them toward my partner through the office; it was a long walk to the creative section of the office.

The office sits in Portobello underneath an arch, so you can hear the overground trains rattle past every couple of minutes; the office itself was a stereotype.

Not a single office block, open plan, some bean bags, the classic football table, great big glass windows, terribly unnecessary surround sound system, a central indoor balcony with a spiral staircase that leads to a raised platform with one large circular table beneath it, and finally a sleep pod that no one was allowed to use.

The indoor balcony served as a watchtower for the creative directors, strategists and marketing seniors. They reigned over the lowly middleweights who worked directly beneath on top of the raised platform, never too far from receiving direct orders. The creative directors placed them there so they could quickly dish out any commands or punishments to the juniors and placement teams.

The lowly juniors clung in groups of fours around the six duo middleweight teams and scurried around and amongst them like little helper ants below them, writing hundreds of lines of copy and scamping hundreds of poster ideas for brands that would never buy the work because those very same almighty creative directors who watched so smugly from their high tower were also the very same individuals who initially ruined advertising's reputation when they were railing lines, chugging champagne, flicking cigarettes into office ashtrays, pinching secretaries inappropriately and telling brands brashly that their ideas are all wrong despite knowing fractionally less about that very same brand, that they should listen to them.

As I walk in, I have to take note of all these factors; you don't want to stand out too much, or they force you to write banner ads for websites. As I look up, two creative directors look out at the office, squinting their eyes and looking for middleweights to do their bidding. I catch eyes briefly with a middleweight strategist who undoubtedly wants me to do some sort of work that she was meant to do, but before she could lock in, I bent down to tie my shoelace.

I look around the office from left to right and stand and walk again toward the junior creatives on the left of the platform; I know if we make eye contact again, whatever awful TikTok, Instagram, or banner brief was on that iPad will be given to me.

I can't today write three hundred lines trying to convince people to let us steal their online information; I can't do it; I have too much on my mind. I want to see if I can show my face, present my deck of blag-able ideas and slink out at lunch for a five-hour walk home.

I spot my art director, Naomi, across the room; she's sitting just under the balcony, out of the watchful eyes of the CDs; you only sit there if you've got something to hide. I can see what she's hiding—the evidence of a big weekend scattered amongst and around her, head buried behind a laptop, her eyes bloodshot, the occasional grimace, five empty cups of coffee spread around her, a pack of Amber Leaf armed at her side.

"What's up, hombre," I say in her general direction whilst waving violently at the other three junior teams scattered along this large work table. We were hungover together now; we had a united front. The vultures dispersed to print posters and get coffee.

Naomi unplugs an AirPod and raises her fist to spud me. We spud. "What's up, playboy?" she says in her accentuated Brooklyn accent. "Tough love, playgirl."

"Tough love, too."

This was how we greeted each other if it was a big weekend; tough love meant it was going to be a long and arduous day.

Naomi and I met at advertising school; she was the only person in the school with a good fashion sense, a thirst for alcohol and a complete disregard for the teachers' advice; in fact, in every single presentation she ever gave, she had only prepared for an hour before but pitched it as she had practised for months. She was a natural, charming, pretty, working class from Brooklyn, New York, hot and fucked more girls than me, did more drugs and somehow did all this being two years younger than me.

Everyone wanted to hire her; for starters, she was a woman, which in a mainly male industry helped with getting a foot in the doors. Secondly, she was mixed race, which helped with the other unfortunate element of the industry, which is that it is almost exclusively white, but the best thing about Naomi was that she knew all the things I stated above, and she played the game to her strengths. "What's the plan?" I say, unloading my work laptop from a locker beside her. "Clean up the deck by nine forty-five, meet at ten forty-five, present an idea each until finish eleven forty-five, go for a long walk at twelve-thirty, and never come back again."

"Sounds like a plan."

A meeting at ten is a death sentence; it means you have to work on Sunday. Sundays are not for hangovers if you are Naomi and I, which means we had to wake up at six a.m. on Monday and hustle for four hours.

Naomi Downs is about five-foot, black American, chain-smokes five cigarettes before coming on a tough love Monday; she calls it "her process"; I call it "the bomb".

The coffee is gasoline, and the cigarette a match.

This is where Naomi gets her energy from, so I say nothing. I watch from afar, amazed, bewildered, in awe.

The brief we had to prepare was for a vegan ice cream company, and the tone of voice was described to us by the strategist as "Fun, fruity and weird". This was a brief from hell, with not a single redeeming quality about it; we didn't even get to try the yoghurt.

All we were armed with were four words: Toffee, Yoghurt, Fun, Weird.

Combined, that probably spells hell.

If a brand describes itself as fun, it means that they suck. Fun isn't a personality trait, and advertising uses the word fun very liberally—too liberally.

After writing sixty lines and Naomi art-directing about twenty posters, we combined efforts—my lines and her designs.

As I wrote the thank-you slide at the end, we were called in for a creative review with three other teams.

We looked from left to right at the three teams, and they were all exhausted, sweating and nervous. For a lot of these teams, their entire existence at the agency was based on them sucking up to creative directors, buying them apples in the mornings, getting to the office two hours early, and leaving three hours late, and for what?

A vegan ice cream brand to get a shitty line of copy that they would put on a billboard somewhere no one would see. They were a disgrace to the human race; Naomi and I knew what this was; it was a good temporary gig; it wasn't the kind of thing you did and told your friends about. It's the kind of job you do until you can't feel anymore, trudging away; not sure if you could have ever made it if you went fully creative.

The first two teams went before us; they looked like an advert for Urban Outfitters or H&M, and they smiled enthusiastically and presented their ideas as though everything that came out of their mouths was gold; the sheer mediocrity of the presentation—and don't get me wrong, I'm no advertising purist, I don't care about the industry even remotely, and I'm no copy god—but to force myself to pretend to be enthusiastic when saying something as ridiculous as "Mmmhhhm, a mouthgasm" to a group of

grown-ups in a room is not something I can do or even externally respect. The meeting chimed on, and the teams vomited out
loosely coherent lines of copy like:

"Where flavour meets enjoyment."

"Follow your tongue."

"You'll be jealous of your tongue."

"Salivation guaranteed."

The creative director assigned to this brief was only still in
advertising for the money; he swiped through his phone and occasionally said "Great job" as though it were playing on a loop. He
didn't care about any of our ideas; we all knew in his pocket was a
loose receipt with some squiggled writing on it that had the actual line he was going to take to the client the next day.

We were to go last; we had about thirty minutes before we
were to present, which was just long enough for us to combine
our creative intelligence to entertain us. Naomi sat across the table, and WhatsApp messaged me through her laptop to mine. We
did this often; it made these meetings bearable.

A message pops up on my laptop.

NAOMI: You know that girl I've been seeing?

COURTNEY: Yeah, the one at Oxford. (NOT BROOKS)

NAOMI: She knows who's going to win the Nobel Prize in
Literature.

An idea pops up in my head; I look up, and Naomi's green
eyes spark with fire; we are sharing a great idea, and I can feel it.
Almost exactly at the same time, we message each other.

BOTH: WE SHOULD PLACE A BET!!

We both scroll through the web, scouring the darkest edges
to find gambling sites that allow you to bet on the most degenerate competitions possible. Our fingers were tapping furiously,
tapping so vigorously that we had both forgotten we were in a
meeting.

"What are you doing?"

The creative director stops the meeting, and for a moment, we both debate internally whether we should be honest; we look at one another and then back at the CD.

"Finishing touches on the deck," I say with my work smile. He scoffs, "A bit late, isn't it?"

I internally shout, "WANKER!" but externally say, "We just want it to be the best version possible."

He rolls his eyes, goes back on his phone and waves with his hand for the current team of slaves to continue presenting.

Naomi sends another message.

"I SENT YOU ONE HUNDRED QUID; IT'S ON UNIBETS. WE HAVE TEN MINUTES BEFORE THE WINNER IS ANNOUNCED."

I put two hundred on Abdulrazak Gurnah. We waited; fingers were crossed under the tables.

"Courtney, Naomi, let's see what you've got?" the CD says.

We stood up and began to rattle off lines into the soundless, airless vacuum that is the pitch room; not a single head in the room paid attention. Everyone's heads were buried in their laptops, wishing they were somewhere, anywhere else but here. After a couple of lines pass by, the vocal rhythm of both my and Naomi's voices infiltrate every corner of the room, creating a mutable calmness.

I realise not one person in the room is paying attention to our deck, and an idea pops into my head—what if I just said what I was thinking? What if I just said what I was thinking but did it in this mutable advertising voice?

"MOUTH COCAINE."

Not a single head turned; I watched the room in amazement.

"I CAN'T BELIEVE I GET PAID TO DO THIS."

Naomi giggled in only what I can describe as an American tone.

"WHAT IS HAPPENING TO MY LIFE."

"STRAWBERRY BERRY GOOD."

"STRAWBERRY BERRY BAD FOR BED."

"STRAWBERRY BERRY BAD FOR BED DUVETS."

"STRAWBERRY TONGUE DUVETS."

Pause; the CD looks up slowly. Naomi and I shrink.

Once again, I've pushed it, and now we are both going to get sacked. Naomi gives me a look whilst shrugging her shoulders that says:

"We had a good run."

The CD's face tenses, and he looks down, his rage beginning to confuse even himself.

"THAT'S IT!" the CD exclaimed, to our surprise.

"You've fucking cracked the brief; that's the line; yeah, it's the perfect amount of weird and fun and kooky."

"It is... No, you're right, it is," Naomi says, writing the line on a slide for the room to see.

I turn around and look at the screen; a notification pops up on the top left of Naomi's work screen.

BBC NEWS: ABDULRAZAK GURNAH WINS NOBEL LITERARY PRIZE....

I can't help but let out a:

"This is the best moment ever."

The CD looks my way—surprised, suspicious even—but ultimately happy that we got the job done.

"Naomi, we fucking did it; we finally won."

Naomi is speechless, on the verge of tears even; we high-five ferociously and repetitively.

To the eye of anyone in that room that day, it either looked as though we were the two biggest advertising nerds that London had to offer or the two worst winners London had to offer. Either way, we both won five thousand pounds, and things were looking up.

"The universe favours idiots."

CHAPTER 11

The nurse came in with a black Percy bag and opened it in front of me.

She then began to screw the large pointy needle onto a vial to make a syringe that looked big enough to kill a horse.

The doctor noticed my discomfort.

"Keep on telling me your stories," he said rather patronisingly.

I focused back on the timeline. "Anyways, a couple of days…

AFTER OUR LUCKY STUNT

Our creative director decided that we were the best junior team suited to come to an advertising award show. There are a couple of clear reasons for this; once again, Naomi being black and a woman is essentially like the agency bringing an award to an award ceremony, and on top of that, somehow, some way, some of our work had been nominated for an award.

Before we get to the proceedings of the night, let me make something crystal clear to you: if you thought I had very little respect for agency life or advertising as a profession, I do.

However, whilst I slander advertising down to its deep, dark capitalist core, I will also say that some of the most creative, intelligent and lovely people I have ever met work in it.

That being said, advertising award shows are some of the stupidest affairs I have ever had the pleasure of witnessing. They are brilliant.

There are a couple of quite strange nuances about advertising awards. Let's begin with what advertising is.

In its simplest form, it attracts attention to a brand, service or business. By that logic, advertising awards should go to:

"Who sold the most products for the brand, service or business that hired them?"

That is not what advertising awards are.

They are, unfortunately, more:

"Who got their client to spend the most money on their personal film."

Everyone knows it; it's not news, it's simply just the way it is; the only difference is now the big brands have caught on, so the awards given are quite underwhelming. I mean, Godzilla is in a Wagamama advert. The creative director metaphorically sucked the dick of whomever the head of marketing was and, in doing so, was allowed to make a three-million-pound, five-minute Godzilla short film that has pretty much nothing to do with advertising.

So why celebrate it?

Here's the kicker: they celebrate what they can get away with. The cheeky bastards—you've got to love it.

In the week leading up to the award shows, I could hear every middle to senior creative in the agency complaining about how irrelevant and pointless advertising awards were.

The classic sentences thrown around the agencies were:

"Award shows are so stupid" and "It's not about the awards."

These statements are usually emitted at a high octave obnoxiously and continuously around the agency.

They bounce off the walls and into everyone's unwilling ears. The truth is they're just scared that they might not win.

Knowing all of these things, Naomi and I were understandably very sceptical of these affairs walking in; we were never the junior team invited to this kind of shindig; it was our fault, of course. I personally would rather sit on a night bus and listen to a drunk homeless man give a speech about where he's going than hear an acceptance speech from an ad exec. But what do I know?

Naomi and I put on our best smart outfits.

A black dress and heels for her and a black tux for me. We hit a pub in Farringdon to have some pints and discuss what we thought the night was going to consist of and, of course, to neck about three pints each so that we came to the party appropriately creative.

I arrived first; the pub I had chosen was an old one in Farringdon, one of those old city pubs protected by the government (rightfully so), a suit pub. For casual after-work drinkers, everyone was over the age of twenty-five, and I'm assuming from the corporate attire that everyone there worked in finance. I walked around assessing the varnished walls and creaky floors. There was a faint smell of beer being emitted from beneath the floorboards, but it didn't bother me; it was familiar, and I felt comfortable. There are some places and things that are just brilliant, places where ideas flow, speeches are given, drinks are drunk, sex begins, love ends, you make friends, have fights, late nights and small bites.

The pub is that place; what would England be without pubs? I can't help but enjoy the smell of stale pub air and smile when I order a pint of Guinness from a big fat bloke who probably thinks I'm a poncey wanker. I am happy here; things are simple—you come here, you say your piece with a friend or a stranger, and you leave to go to the next place. Free therapy.

"Hey, buddy," I can hear a distinctly American voice piercing the air of the pub and immediately splitting the crowd into those who like and do not like Yanks.

"You all right, Naomi?" I respond.

"I'm in heels, Courtney; I'm the furthest thing from fucking all right that you can be."

She always says my name when addressing me; I never really understood why, but I have noticed that Americans do it more than English people.

"Two pints of Guinness, please, good sir." Naomi tries to imitate an English accent for the fat barman.

He is unamused; I am very amused.

We quickly neck about three pints each and begin the walk to where the award show is.

Across the road, we can see some people dressed in similar attire to us.

"Corporate or marketing?" Naomi says as we find cover behind a car and wait for them to pass by.

"Marketing for sure."

For context, marketing thinks everyone in creative is a ditzy dreamer, and everyone in the creative department believes that marketers are useless. This generally causes animosity and awkward conversation between groups.

We quickly creep across the road and slink behind them, hidden shadows ready to reveal our true colours once inside the award show.

As we followed them, Naomi would hide behind a pillar and provide cover whilst I would move to a car close to them, and then vice versa.

The mission was to see if we could get to the award show without being spotted. They were completely oblivious, stuck in their childish conversations about the future and having a steady job blah blah blah.

"Courtney, Naomi, what are you guys doing?"

It turns out that Marketing was not as stupid as we thought; our cover was blown, and now we had to go into work mode.

To give you insight, work mode is when you converse at about sixty per cent of what your real personality is, leaving out swear words, political views, strong opinions, where you grew up, what your friends are like, how many drinks you've had, whether you use drugs, how often you holiday and anything in between.

You are essentially left with about three conversational topics to choose from: the weather, which is always shit; what beer you are drinking; and, of course, work chat, which no one on earth wants to talk about but, unfortunately, is the only thing you have in common.

"So what do you think the chances of winning an award are?" I say into the open air, hoping to start a generic conversation I can then slink out of.

"Best copy probably, most creative agency and best-directed TV commercial," someone from Marketing responds.

"Nice, nice."

Naomi and I drop the pace of our walk as the crowd overtakes us.

The award is at a great hall in the City of London; Marketing is dressed efficiently and similarly. The creatives, on the other hand, stick out like sore thumbs; they're usually younger, wearing trainers, the odd polka-dot tie, ill-fitting blazer jackets and beards or eccentric haircuts. The hall is filled with great archways, coats of arms, champagne trays and suspiciously long queues to the bathroom. Proper castle stuff.

Our agency has our section etched out right in front of the stage next to Sky, Channel 4, ITV, Netflix and Paramount. The faraway stage has a Z-list celebrity standing on it, ready to give out awards. Gemma is something or other from some show like Big Brother. As you look around at one of these affairs, it is almost impossible to take them seriously. If you are there, you're essentially going to get an award, but just for context, let me give you some of the awards you can win and the real translation of what they mean.

Best cinematic: what this means is who has the most money to pay for a real director.

Best low-budget: what this means is which show was good enough to succeed even though the advertising agency spent no money on marketing it to the world.

Best high-budget: in the literal sense of the word, this means who spent the most money.

Most creative agency: which agency is most likely to trick a client into spending large sums of money for no reason on their ideas (I respect this one).

Best copy or art direction: what did they let you get away with?

Naomi and I sit at a round table—you know, like one of the ones you see at the Golden Globes—except instead of Brad Pitt or a Francis Ford Coppola, you're sitting next to Dan from IT, who, despite his misguided excitement, is a lovely bloke.

Shout out to Dan if you're reading this, absolute stellar guy. Naomi, Dan and I down a bunch of champagne on an empty stomach as the award show begins. The first award goes to Sky, and they play the advert that wins.

The advert is of a cow jumping over a fence, and the award is for creativity.

Now, I am not a genius, I am not, and I don't pretend to be, but to say that a cow jumping over a fence is creative is surely taking liberties with creativity itself.

The conversation about this cow and this fence being creative went a little like this. Jeremy, a middleweight creative on the table:

"It's about the curve of the jump and what the fence represents."

I heard this comment and thought there was no conceivable way that he believed that.

Why not indulge?

"What does that fence represent?" I ask.

"Well, it's about the switch from traditional milk to oat milk; you see, the cow is escaping the farm, leaving us, the traditional milk-consuming demographic, with only oat milk... the cow isn't working for us anymore. He's free."

Everyone at the table nods in agreement. I blink in shock.

"No, you're right, Jeremy; I didn't think of it like that."

I am now one hundred per cent certain that no one in this room is real.

This is a video game, and Jeremy is the main character, which means that I'm a side quest, and he's set the difficulty of the game too easy.

I've often wondered, as I'm sure many of you have also wondered, what would happen if you just treated life like a video game?

If advertising was a video game, it would be about problem-solving, and every problem solved, you'd reach the next level along the way, collecting more armour and special abilities. To break it down further, the problem would be whatever a brand wants from you; the level up would be to win an award, and the trophy or armour would be a pay rise.

"Hey, hey, Courtney," Naomi pokes my shoulder rudely, interrupting my extremely important daydream.

"Yeah, what?"

Behind me, at a nearby table, I can hear a Netflix marketing team faintly talk; Naomi can hear the conversation too and suggests with her eyes that I should avert my attention from Jeremy and zone out with her toward this group of American account men.

I oblige, leaning back on my chair and letting Jeremy explain to the rest of the table his growing thesis on the curve of the cow's jump.

"Yo bro, look at this chick," a very loud, slick Asian—and I'm assuming Netflix account man—said brashly behind me.

"She looks like a tranny, bro," another almost identical but Caucasian finance bro responds.

"I'd still smash, though, bro," the final and third obnoxious finance bro adds, fidgeting clearly from cocaine consumption.

Out of nowhere, Naomi adds from our table, leaning in, "Show me the chick."

The finance bros are taken aback; they've rarely dealt with a woman challenging them in their court; they feel uncomfortable at first, all of them looking at one another and agreeing in unison through their body language whether they're about to be exposed or if this is a genuine reaction.

The Caucasian one slowly gives Naomi the phone and awaits her approval. They show Naomi the girl's Instagram page.

Time goes by slowly, and I grit my teeth.

Naomi takes a deep breath in, then slowly exhales.

Then quickly responds by clicking her thumb and index finger together and saying, "Would smash, would smash." Bro's language for very good.

They respond as a group with smiles of approval. Naomi hands the phone back.

I can see my creative director and middleweights heading out of the hall for a cigarette.

I contemplate following, but I'm much safer here drunk where my opinionated opinions stay between Dan, Naomi and these finance bros.

The next award comes along for best copy-written poster; Naomi and I joke with one another at the idea that our "strawberry tongue duvets" line could win an award.

"Imagine that; how ridiculous would that be, how utterly stupid, how hilarious, how good would that be for our careers?"

"THE AWARD GOES TO IMAGINE THAT CREATIVE FOR THEIR VEGAN ICE CREAM ADVERTISEMENT POSTER AND STRAPLINE!"

I didn't know that you could be disappointed in a good way, but it's possible. Our line was scattered amongst some much better ones on the screen, but it was there.

"IS THERE ANYONE FROM IMAGINE THAT CREATIVE HERE TO RECEIVE THE AWARD?"

In advertising, if you are a junior and you've come up with an idea, generally, the creative director takes the credit, and you get a pay rise in the form of a job offer from somewhere else, which in advertising means a pay rise.

A few more seconds passed, and not one of the two hundred IMAGINE THAT employees got out of their seats.

I looked at Naomi, and I knew, I just knew at that moment, that this was it; this was one of the most important moments of my life; I wasn't going to get a pay rise, a job offer, or even get to keep the award. No, I was going to get something far better—the perfect Instagram picture. All the possibilities: imagine the family conversations about how well I'm doing and the girls—think of what the girls would think.

The spirit that carried me up that hill in Thailand was back, and it had energy, virility and... I was making my way around the tables, smiling and waving at the camera.

I could see myself on the big screen.

I walked past all the IMAGINE THAT employees as they thought to themselves:

"Who is he?"

"If he was going to win an award, why was his table so far at the back of the hall?"

Honestly, the walk from my table to the stage genuinely took about four minutes, but hey, more air time for me.

I briefly looked behind; Naomi had stayed seated. Fine, that didn't bother me.

I was going to feel how it felt to win, and although I had very little to do with this award, this was a first, and I was going to cherish it.

My chest puffed, my work smile gleaming.

Five paces away, four paces away, three paces away.

Gemma, the Z-list celebrity, was unsure who I was but handed me the award regardless.

I'm holding the gold award; it's of Atticus holding a brain over his head. I look down at it and analyse it; I think to myself out loud:

"That's fucking stupid."

Except I said that into a mic representing an entire company of over one thousand five hundred industry professionals.

The crowd is silent.

I smile, remembering you can say anything with a smile.

I am meant to give a speech, except I don't have a speech, but there is one thing I know.

If there was one Jeremy on my table, there was one Jeremy on every table.

Cough cough

The camera zooms in on my face.

The thought comes to me, a well-known advertising technique to sell an idea: MEMORABLE,

TRUTHFUL

AND MOTIVATING.

I have to say something no creative would ever say whilst up here.

I let the room settle, the claps fade, and the room breathes...

"I couldn't have done this without Marketing or the strategists, which tells you all you need to know about how I feel about this award."

I salute the finance bros and the marketing department.

I walk down from the stage to the only person I can remember from Marketing to give her the award, walk back to my table, and sit down.

"You are going to get fired," Naomi remarks.

I am unflustered; I had bigger fish to fry than vegan ice cream. I didn't learn much from that.

The nurse asked me if I wanted to take off my shirt for the procedure. She held the syringe in the air.

"I didn't want to."

"Come on, Courtney, almost done now."

She dabbed a cotton swab in ethanol and rubbed my arm with it.

"You are the second person who was willing to pay a thousand pounds to get this done early today."

"A dying breed," I retorted.

"Indeed."

I looked up at the nurse; her eyes were happily focused on the needle; she was enjoying this far too much.

CHAPTER 12

"I COULD SEE SOLL'S HEAD"

Bopping and weaving in and amongst the crowd, rising and falling as it made its way through Borough Market toward me.

"Oi, oi, oi!" he shouted from about ten metres away. "Look here; it's Mister Advertising."

He is, of course, referring to a picture I posted on my Instagram of me holding a slightly bronzed-looking golden trophy award.

"I've got a plan," he said.

Soll hadn't been coming out as much; he looked healthier and more lively, as though his life was coming together well.

So naturally, I told him he looked well, and he didn't flinch, which is annoying because that means I'm not the only person who's been telling him that.

"Where are we going?"

Soll smiled in a way that meant trouble, and he started to walk away, leading me out of the market and onto the Borough High Street, down a side road, up some stairs, through a council estate, down some stairs out of a council estate until we got to a place called "Jasmine Thai Massage". It sat at the bottom of a large brutalist estate, between a fish and chips shop and a tanning salon.

The building was rough around the edges; it looked dated, the type of thing you see everywhere in London, but you never really get used to. That was this place—the kind of place that the new London was leaving behind.

Everything around it was stark: one empty road with an empty ice cream van, no people, just frosted store windows, a couple of suspicious-looking juvenile drug dealers and us.

"Well, my friend, what are we doing?" I asked, going along with the whole thing but rather confused about what we were doing.

He looks at the massage parlour as if that were the answer to my question.

"We have reached the Garden of Eden; this is it. It may not look like much, but this is all you'll ever need to get through the winter months: a massage parlour, a tanning bed and... the cinema, but you already knew that one."

I am very confused.

"Right, mate, all I see is a shit massage parlour, a tanning salon, three juvenile delinquents and a chippy," I remark, confused because it appears to him that we are looking at two completely separate things.

"First, we tan," Soll says, walking into a tanning salon that both looks and feels like a front for some kind of money-laundering scheme.

Soll looks from left to right and then runs to the door, leaving me standing in the stark cold air alone in my parka.

I am still extremely confused as to whether I'm meant to follow him or whether I'm meant to stay here and wait.

The tanning salon door opens a crack, and Soll looks at me, pokes his head out from left to right, then mouths:

"RUN," whilst gesturing with his hand that I should run toward him. So I look left to right, take my hands out of my parka and run in. The frosted door opens up, and I tumble in.

The interior is pink; there are four pods lined against the walls, and the odd classic palm tree poster is hung up on the walls.

A large orange bodybuilder lady stands next to the door behind a small blue desk. She seems to know Soll pretty well, which I can tell by the way that she isn't bothered at all by his presence.

The lady scans me; her neck muscles flex, and she looks shiny, as though her skin were made from dark brown latex.

I am a foreigner, a trespasser, a noob; it's her territory, and I am someone to be cautious of.

Soll walks ahead to one of the pods. He undresses down to a rainbow-print Speedo, pulls out some UV goggles and places them on his forehead with his hands on his hips.

I am very confused.

"You got something to tell me, Soll?" I chirp to him.

He pays no mind.

The orange lady circles me, looking me up and down, occasionally leaning in to assess my skin, my face and, for all accounts, my character.

"Soll, what are we doing here?"

The lady hands me a board with registration details on it.

"This is the answer, man; this is it," he says in my general direction as I fill in the details.

He begins to pace around a solitary bench in the middle of the store.

"So why do we go out so much in winter?" He pauses and lifts his hand, gesturing for me to answer the question.

"Because winter in London is fucking horrible?" I remark.

"Why's it so horrible?" he responds.

"It's cold; everyone looks ugly, and seasonal depression is a rampant disease that enters the system around November and can't be cured until late April."

"But you know who's never ugly in winter?"

"Girls?"

"EXACTLY!!"

His pacing becomes more frantic.

"Courtney, I have found out that all the girls that we see are hitting tanning beds throughout the winter."

"So?"

"We are going to even the playing field."

The large orange lady holds up a zebra Speedo and matching goggles in my peripheral vision.

Soll opens his pod and tells me that he's going to see me in fifteen minutes.

I look over to the orange lady and then back at the pod and think to myself: this is like drugs; this is what we do; this is our problem; we find shortcuts; it's our greatest talent; it's the thing that makes us unique. There is no corner we aren't willing to cut. Brilliant.

The lady showed me how it worked; there was a button with

a light symbol on it; it looked a bit like a nuclear bomb, which didn't fill me with lots of confidence considering.

"BLUETOOTH," the orange lady says extremely loudly in a thick Russian accent and directly into my right ear.

I thought this quite a self-damaging affair, so I appropriately played the Stone Roses' "Fools Gold" to romanticise the moment.

Plus, the song is nine minutes and fifty-three seconds long, seven seconds shorter than my ten-minute tanning bed session.

As the pod closed, the lady informed me that I could be completely naked in the tanning bed.

If I were lying on a nude beach in France and there was no cool draft, sure, I'd keep my piece out, but to intentionally let UV rays hit my cock...

Well, this was going to take some serious debate.

On the one hand, having a full-body tan meant that in the event that this sunbed worked and we were more tanned, we would be more attractive essentially (by European standards, of course), allowing us to get laid more often.

Then perhaps being browner on all fronts was better.

But on the other hand, frying my genitals in what is basically a microwave felt disingenuous to the overall mission of having more sex.

Once in the pod, you will be surrounded by a blue light, the doors will close you in, and your body will begin to heat up.

Throughout this experience, you will ask yourself: surely this cannot be good for me.

But don't think those thoughts; keep your eyes on the end goal, keep your eyes on the prize.

After the set ten minutes finish.

You will hear a loud ding; that ding signifies that you are now ready for consumption.

The doors will open, and you'll leave a new man, a darker man, a man who looks healthy.

Outside of the pod is a large mirror in the hallway; as the doors opened, I could see Soll standing in front of it, flexing his nonexistent muscles in the mirror.

I walked over and began to do the same.

There are two things that I noticed immediately. To begin with, I was very tired—tired in that I had been in the sun too long way—and secondly, my skin was the same shade of pale white that it was ten minutes prior.

"Soll, I still look fucking see-through. How am I going to get laid if I'm still see-through?"

"It's like going to the gym, mate. You've got to put in the work."

Against my better judgment, for some reason, that made perfect sense to me. So, I booked another session two days later.

We redressed and left. "What now?" I asked.

Soll smiled a smile that scared me. "Vanilla Thai Massage."

I learnt that tanning beds are addictive.

"I think I know where this is going," the doctor said, revealing to both the nurse and me that he, too, is a degenerate.

"SOLL AND I ROCKED OUT OF THE TANNING SALON:

Bursting with energy—or at least Soll was; honestly, I was very underwhelmed by the experience. So underwhelmed that I decided to commit to a monthly subscription.

Now, unbeknownst to me, it turns out that every single massage parlour with a "Vanilla" or a "Jasmine" or a "Mint" or any kind of adjective in the title is a happy-ending massage parlour.

I had no idea that this was a thing, no idea whatsoever.

Soll and I walked in and asked for a thirty-minute massage each.

To wit, they responded, "Cash only." A smarter man would've seen that as a sign that this was not an establishment with integrity. But hey, integrity is hard to find these days, so I thought to myself, let's give 'em a shot.

The second sign that this was not a serious establishment was that Soll wanted me to try it. Soll is an extremely wealthy Jewish boy from Hampstead who wouldn't be caught dead in south London unless he somehow gained something out of it.

"I don't have any cash," I said to an uninterested Asian lady sitting behind the counter.

"I've got this," Soll responded. This was suspicious, too.

But free money is easy money, and I am not one to turn something of that nature down.

The third sign that something was going on was that Soll handed the moody Asian lady one hundred and twenty pounds instead of the sixty that was meant to cover the two of us.

Soll patted me on the back. "I'll see you on the other side."

He then began to walk down a long dark hallway, lit with fairy lights, until his figure faded into the darkness.

The lady behind the counter then waved her hand slowly to follow down the passage, and into the darkness, I could hear a door open ahead of me. "Darkness be gone!" he exclaimed and then shut a door behind him.

Now, at this particular moment, I was certain of where this was going—not fully certain, but slightly sure of the direction.

And yet my curiosity, my dick, or both followed the fairy lights down the dark hall. A hand reached out to me at the end of the dark hall.

And with it, a calm voice said: "Come in."

I stripped down to my boxers.

"No, all your clothes," the voice said from the dark corner.

I knew what I was about to do; this was to be a new low, a low that I honestly didn't need to reach, but that thing inside, the thing that excites you because you know it's wrong, that thing— it overpowers all reason.

And yet, you can always say no the first time; it's the only time you have a can. But on this particular occasion, the way I saw it was that I wasn't paying. I rationalised my next actions under the pretext that Soll was the one funding my interests in hedonistic activities.

So, let me take you through the process; let me bring you into the darkness with me.

The massage begins, and you're face down, completely naked, and then a masseuse applies an entire bottle of oil to your back. I mean, the amount of baby oil used for this massage is quite unnecessary.

So after the masseuse covers your entire body—emphasis on the entire body—a rather unsanitary dialogue begins; it usually goes a little like as follows.

"Do you work out?" she says.

I reply, "Of course." I am lying.

Then her comments and her hands begin to get lower, like really low, like nobody's butt holds that much tension low.

Now, as a twenty-one-year-old man, I'd like to tell you that I got up outraged by her advances, shocked and scared at the direction this message was going.

But that's not in line with my twenty-twenty-one philosophy, is it?

"Turn over," she said. Now, to be completely honest, the lady who was giving me a massage was, in all parts, not the most attractive lady.

Now illuminated by a red lava lamp in the corner of the room.

I could see her; she was wrinkled, weathered and old. Her make-up cracked and crumbled as she smiled at me.

"Your friend comes here a lot."

"No surprise there," I muttered awkwardly because my cock was out.

"Have you been here before?"

I was offended by this because I assume the kind of individuals who frequent these places don't have my dashing looks or evident charm.

So I sternly said "No" in defiance.

Now, to go further into the details of this interaction would be honestly quite disgusting, so instead, I'm going to give you a poetic description.

It's like getting a really, really, almost better-than-sex massage but on your dick.

So, instead of going in-depth about various rhythms, strokes and verbal quotes, once I was made aware of the existence of these places, I did some research online.

It's fucking amazing. Google a dodgy name like "Jasmine Mint Massage" and look at the reviews.

Usually, there will be one Karen and another bloke who have both accidentally gone to the parlour with different experiences.

The first thing you want to look for is the Karen comment. It will go a little something like this:

"This is not a real establishment; the massage was a light rub; I was then offered 'other additional' services that I refused. DO NOT GO HERE!!!"

She will rate it one star; she might even mention in the comments that if she could, she would rate it no stars.

On the other hand, a bloke named Mike will have stumbled upon this particular parlour and will have commented also.

His comment will look a little bit like this:

"Stumbled into this place by chance. Best massage of my life; ask for Lemon when you are in there." He will have inevitably added a weird kind of sexual emoji at the end and rated the parlour five stars.

Because of these two opposing forces, just like nature, the ratings will balance each other out.

So most, if not all, massage parlours have a three-star rating; anything lower, and it's very, very bad, and anything more, and it's probably a professional establishment.

The professional massage came to an end; I was left feeling empty, honestly, so I quickly put my clothes on and ran out of the parlour. On the way out, I heard: "Come again soon."

Soll was sitting on a bench across the street, smoking a cigarette, looking up at planes in the sky.

I shivered as a cold wind blew through me.

I put my hands in my pockets, tensed up and ran across the street to sit next to him.

"We have reached the end of our voyage, mate," Soll said, blowing smoke and oxygen into the cold air.

"Oh, have we?" I respond jovially.

"Courtney, I wanted to tell you something, and I thought this the best way."

"You're gay; everyone knows, and we don't mind," I interrupted him.

"Hilarious. No, I'm flying to New York tomorrow."

My heart sank a bit; it was always us against the shit. No matter how low or high I'd go, Soll was always there by my side, making it an adventure adding his light personality.

"Oh…" I looked down.

"Courtney, you can't do this forever; eventually, you're going to have to grow up and take your job and life seriously."

"Have you told Greeny or Greeny?"

"Fuck them. When I leave, get some new friends, people that are doing stuff, and hit the gym or write a novel or something."

Well, there's a thought.

"When do you leave?"

"I'm getting there for Christmas."

"Ah, fuck, what am I gonna do without you?" I said, laughing at the reality of the statement.

Soll smiled at me and flicked his cigarette at a nearby drain with sick on it. Missed, and pointed across the street to the massage parlour.

"When in doubt, look for a happy ending."

We went out drinking that night—from the Brixton to King's Cross, from King's Cross to Baker Street, from Baker Street to Mayfair and finally from Mayfair to Shoreditch.

The whole night reminiscing on all the fun we'd had, all the bad behaviour and even some of the good.

We ended up back at my apartment chatting with two girls. I knew I had work tomorrow, but I didn't care.

This was more important anyway.

One of the girls played "Viva Las Vegas", and Soll and I danced around the room singing the lyrics.

"I'm gonna keep on the run.

I'm gonna have some fun.

If it costs me my very last dime

If I wind up broke, oh well.

I'll always remember that I had a swingin' time."

"Viva Las Vegas"

"PLAY IT AGAIN!"

"Viva Las Vegas"

And again and again and again.

The lesson I learnt there is that a good happy ending usually involves a hand job.

The nurse looked at me, thoroughly displeased with the story.

The doctor laughed.

"How many have you had already?" she asked.

"I'm just missing one."

She plunged the syringe into a vial and pulled the liquid out into the syringe.

Then she placed it on the table in front of the doctor and insinuated with her eyes that he should make this as painful for me as possible.

"Courtney, don't look at the needle. Look at me and tell me about the girl."

He came over to me and wiped my shoulder with the alcohol, and cuffed my shirt. I winced.

CHAPTER 13

"SOLL LEFT FOR NEW YORK THE NEXT DAY."

I came into work three hours late and cried in a cubicle, not because Soll left, although that didn't help. I was crying in the toilet because, as a punishment for my award speech, Naomi and I had been put on a vegan cat food brief.

They wanted us to get vegans to make their cats eat vegan, too. My issue with it was that cats are carnivores. But that wasn't the reason I was crying, either.

Have you ever been so viscerally hungover to the point where every morsel of your being is in pain?

No amount of Panadol, Valium, coffee or jerking off could remove this pain. And you realise it's not a hangover; it's something incurable.

This wasn't a hangover. Advertising had finally gotten to me; I had lost my lust for life, and I was suffering from a bad case of existential dread.

Janet, the seventy-year-old secretary, was no longer a sweet old lady. No, Janet was me in seventy years if I kept on this path.

It was time to make a change. So, I tried to go sober.

Being sober is admirable, but it's a bit like you've just got an incurable disease. All of the people you used to drink and do drugs with give you pitiful smiles. Everyone you know looks at the non-alcoholic beers you are drinking, and they say:

"Well done, I'm proud of you." Or: "I don't know how you find the willpower." What they're really saying is: "We can't hang out anymore", "You're not like me", and "You make me feel bad about myself."

The funny thing is, it's similar to having incurable cancer; at the beginning, around seven or eight p.m. the night you can hang out, you are still one of the boys, and the girls don't notice a lack of confidence or energy. In fact, you can tell people, "I'm sober", and depending on how far you may have previously pushed the boat out being not sober, they'll reply genuinely impressed.

The beginning of the night is the ascension: everyone has had one or two drinks. They're honestly just a bit more interesting to talk to, and it's still an enjoyable night. When you get to around nine, usually the men are worse than the girls; they're all looking for liquid courage, and being sloppy is just a necessary side effect. Around this time, too, the boys begin to lose composure, and later, usually around eleven, the girls do too. I hadn't noticed it at all before, but it seems that even when drunk, most girls are conscious of it, whereas, in men, consciousness is merely an afterthought—something like a mosquito flying past your ear once every couple of minutes, a pint can easily squash it.

Once you've gotten past nine-thirty, you're in the danger zone, and that danger zone comes in the form of your closest friends.

James had snuck out of the countryside to come down to London for a day. He said it was medical, but I'm pretty sure it's because the only app that works out there is like eHarmony or Bumble.

Anyway, I'm pretty sure that wasn't the reason he came down.

"Oi, Courtney," James drawls from across the table, his arms wrapped around two girls.

"Ye was up," I reply with fake energy, a forced smile and agitated eye contact.

"You suck when you're sober," a statement so casual and yet so hideous and haunting.

"Oh, that's nice."

"No one likes you when you're not drinking. Look at yourself; you're fucking boring."

"How charming you are," I say, now acutely aware of my highly conscious disposition.

"James, how is that project..." My question falls on deaf ears; the alcohol has taken his brain to a happier, more interesting place than this conversation.

"BARTENDER, GET FOUR TEQUILA SHOTS!" James yells at a petite, innocent-looking blonde bartender as she scurries off to prepare the drinks.

If you have ever wanted your mates to buy you free drinks all night, here is the secret: simply tell them you are sober. This works even better for drugs. Drinks will be bought for you everywhere you go by people you know and even people you don't. Why? Two reasons.

1. They want to bring you down to their level. This is common with people who don't have a lot going on in their lives: the unemployed, the trust fund babies, people in marketing, and the pub regulars. They are not drinking to have fun, and they do want you not to have fun with them.
2. They want you to enjoy yourself, and most people, for better or for worse, want you to just have a good time with them, and they think that if you drink, you will—which is true.

Around twelve is when the problems arise, and this is mostly to do with you. My experience has been from the male perspective, so if you are a female, I'm sure the same applies with varying degrees of idiosyncrasy. Your game sober is better—it is—you know exactly what's going on, where and why. So when you talk to a girl, they're impressed mostly because every other guy around you has devolved back to the Palaeolithic period (caveman reference, all you dummies out there).

Talking to your male friends, as you can tell from the above conversation, goes one of two ways: your friends congratulate you but don't want to talk—why would they? You are at a pub, and the purpose of being at a pub is drinking, and the male species, if anything, we are suckers for hypocritical logic. Or it's overtly aggressive, whether that be your friends trying their hardest to slur and spit on you when they're drunk or talking at you mindlessly, saying essentially nothing.

My phone chimes and brings on my biggest sober challenge yet: dating. Dating at twenty-one after COVID-19-19 is amazing;

everyone, and I mean everyone, wants to have unprotected, heinous sex. The kind of sex where the next day you sit butt naked at the end of the bed with your head in your hands, praying that you still have mouthwash. But to get to this level of sex, one must be drunk, scouring the deep dark depths of Hinge, not looking for love, and in dire need of sex—almost so dire it's medical.

My phone vibrates in my pocket as the pub descends further into degeneracy—a Snapchat notification from Amora.

I open my phone bravely and tilt it in a way that no one else can see what I'm reading. I swipe her message bar just enough so that I can see what she's saying but not enough to alert her that I have read the text. This is one of the features of Snapchat that make it optimal for sexting; the messages auto-delete after they've been sent.

Amora: I'm naked

My brain explodes with desire, strategic answers and questions.

God damn.

How do I reply?

I've got a minute to reply.

I'm gonna reply to this; this is a good answer, I think.

Courtney: Time and place?

A couple of minutes go by, and in those minutes, James, who is sitting across this large wooden table, is beginning to make out with these two blonde chicks. The pride in me tells me that if I was drinking, it would be me and not him. Bastard. I can hear a loud sniffing noise to the left of me as Greeny and Soll try to subtly do bumps of cocaine at the table. It's moments like these when you look at your friends for the idiots they are; being sober, if nothing else, is a real slap in the face when it comes to whom you spend your time with.

But that will come later. For now, the pressing matter of sexting whilst completely sober must be accomplished. In my opinion—which is the only opinion you'll be hearing in this book—

sexting sober is similar to doing an algebra test drunk: because the drunk part is great, it's just a shame you're doing an algebra test. The same goes for sober sexting: being sober, good lad; being sober whilst sexting, good luck, lad.

Amora: Don't be so rigid

Amora: That's not very exciting for me.

"WHY ARE WOMEN SO COMPLICATED!!!"

"You what?" Greeny replied.

"Nothing, nothing, snort your drugs, you wrong'un."

Eyes on the prize, eyes on the prize, Courtney; this is all you have left—no alcohol, no drugs, no more late nights. This is what you've got left: sex.

Courtney: I want to rip your clothes off.

Too aggressive? No good start, valiant effort.

Courtney: I want to rip your clothes off and grab you in a sexual way.

In a sexual way, in a fucking sexual way? I don't even want that. Stick with it; females are crazy, and this should work.

Courtney: I want to rip your clothes off and grab you strongly whilst kissing your neck, and I want to fuck you.

Strongly? What the fuck is 'strong'? I cringe with fear.

Courtney: When I see you, I want to rip your clothes off, be a little rough, kiss your neck and fuck you; I've been thinking about it all day. (Sent)

Nice stuff—you are a natural, a master of sexting; I dare say a god of the sext. Now, to wait for her reply, then slip out of the pub and have sex. Brilliant chess move.

What will it take? At most, she'll reply in like thirty minutes; how could she not? We are sexting, and when you sext, you reply quickly because that is the polite thing to do. Forty minutes later, I checked my phone one hundred and three times.

Still no reply. A bead of sweat is forming on my forehead, and my leg, which I tap frequently, is now stomping the ground quickly. This is not ideal; this is bad because I have sent her a text, but she could be in multiple scenarios.

Scenario 1: She and all her friends are reading my sext together, and they're all laughing. Quite bad, but I could play that off easily.

Scenario 2: She is with another guy and is reading my sext out to said other guy, and they're also laughing. Very unsavoury thought.

Scenario 3: She is reposting it on Twitter, and I'm about to get Johnny Depped by the Me Too movement.

These are three of the scenarios that plagued my mind for forty minutes, then an hour, then an hour and a half, then three hours and THEN FIVE FUCKING HOURS.

Just as my mind is on the brink of psychosis, my phone chimes.

Amora on text: Hey, you free tonight?

So she hasn't seen the sext yet. I could delete it. No, this is a test; she wants to see if I can hang if I can make decisions and stick by them—or maybe I'm overthinking.

I am probably overthinking. I'm going to call her; that way, we've had a dialogue between the sext and the message, so if she brings it up, I can play it cool and tell her that it was a joke.

Bring, bring. Bring, bring.

Amora: "Hello, Court," she says slowly and sexy.

"'Ello, 'ello, hello, and how are we?"

"I saw your Snapchat."

My heart pounds. Say something, say something witty to offset the text, but what?

"Oh yeah, and what do you think," I say with a confident tone to mask my fear.

"It wasn't very sexy, but the fact you tried was cute. Do you want to meet up tonight?"

"Why didn't you reply then?" I say, slightly offended and ignoring her advance.

"I wanted to make you sweat," she chuckles.

"I'm not sure if I can make it to the pub; call me after."

Before I could rebut, she hung up the phone. I looked up at James, Ren and Greeny.

Their eyes filled with disgust, and I know why.

"You are fully and wholly dick-whipped!" James shouts. Ren nods in agreement.

I look down at my phone, the sext opened without a reply, no beer in my hand to numb the pain, and then back up at my disappointed, inebriated friends.

"You're right."

"Don't hibernate like last time," said Ren.

"You don't want to get fat again," added James quite unnecessarily.

"They're right, you were a lot less fun, Court," some person I've never had a sober conversation with chimed in from over my shoulder.

"Aww, guys, thanks."

My male support system of friends once again tried their absolute hardest to be as unhelpful as possible.

They proceeded to cause mayhem in and around the pub until we were all abruptly kicked out and then let back in after some sweet talking in the form of fifty quid from James. Ren and Greeny found two lovely old Irish ladies to do cocaine with, which would have been perfectly fine if they hadn't also been the musicians playing live music for the pub that night.

After some convincing by Greeny, they eventually sang an IRA song to the dismay of some older English fellows in the pub who did not find it quite so amusing.

This was, of course, even more amusing.

One of the drunker English men stood up to shout:

"GET THE FUCK OUT!"

The energy in the room was no longer playful; the pub took a deep breath, the occupants scanned one another, and silence filled every square inch of the room. Until the bar erupted with shouts and screams from the Irish band and slurred, incoherent rebuttals from the old English pensioners at the pub after another Irish bloke in the pub threw a half pint of Guinness over my head and into the forming crowd of angry English men, there was no stopping it; glasses were thrown, drinks spilt, slurs said, and eventually punches thrown. James and Greeny stood in the madness between a husband and wife in their thirties, the sparks watching the fire proudly as it consumed the building and everyone in it. Sweet anarchy.

Funnily enough, one of the band members, presumably the coked-up one, continued to play the fiddle, which added a dramatic slow-motion movie feeling to this symphony of violence.

I looked down at the tequila shots. It stared back at me; it knew it was affecting me. It was clear it shouldn't be the answer—but it was; it was. I picked up one of the shiny cylinders and held it in my hand, rubbing the outer glass and smudging my reflection with a thumb. Maybe once more, maybe I'll just have one more drink; why not, I'm young, this is what being twenty-one is about, drinking and having fun with your friends. I catch James's eyes; he would do anything to bring me to his level. He wants me to make the bad decisions so he wasn't alone. In defiance, I flip him off and take the shot; the alcohol burns a hole in my chest.

I look up to see James has moved on, mission complete; he's already trying to destroy a new target, attempting to break up a marriage by kissing both the fiancée and groom.

I'm not that bad, though, not me, not this night; once they leave, I'll change, I wasn't like them when they weren't around. They stood at different ends of the pub, each one screaming, yelling, poking, pestering, philandering, snorting, and burping. I could see them for who they were, all hyper-aware of their terrible effects, and yet they didn't care. I didn't want to see that because I was that too. So I slammed another shot.

"Ding, ding", my phone chimes.

Amora: I can't make it to the pub, but you can meet me at a party tonight if you like.

The smart thing to do here is to wait thirty minutes to make it appear as though you are not that eager. When it comes to the probability of sex, I am rarely smart. Three seconds later.

Courtney: Send me your location, and I'll meet you in an hour.

Amora: It's an event at Shoreditch House.

After texting Amora, I looked around the chaotic pub for my friends so I could say goodbye to them.

James and Ren were joking around with a group of roadmen from the area at the other end of the bar.

The mixture of the two groups was strange; maybe Ren was friends with them because James definitely would not be.

Greeny was next to me; he had unloaded everything out of his wallet. The contents were made up of a few loose receipts, the infamous one-hundred-dollar bill, eight loose Valiums, half a gram of coke in a vial, a full gram of ketamine in a baggy, some kind of Tramadol or OxyContin pill and two blue Tesla ecstasy pills.

Blue Tesla pills are very, very rare.

"How did you get your hands on those, my friend?" I ask, fully aware that this was one of the only topics we shared in common.

Greeny shrugged.

"Well, aren't you quite the conversationalist," I prodded.

Just as he was about to reply, we heard a loud bang coming from the general direction of Ren and James.

I could see it in the reflection of Greeny's eyes already.

Ren was being throttled against the bar by one of the larger roadmen.

Just to make it clear, a roadman is usually but not always a drug dealer and generally someone not worth messing with, often in full tracksuits, wearing black Air Forces and a strapback of sorts. Almost always the anti-social type, although I've met some lovely ones, too.

The roadman was strangling Ren against the bar, his eyes were lit on fire, and it was clear that if he was not stopped, he would kill him.

James and the other slightly fatter, less athletic-appearing roadman were wildly swinging at each other.

Every third punch would land on a shoulder, the front of a forehead, nothing enough to knock the other out but enough to keep James preoccupied whilst Ren was getting strangled.

In true Irish pub fashion, the bystanders around were too busy verbally fighting or lovingly singing to even notice what was going on.

Greeny got up and grabbed me by the shirt to get me up from my now slightly drunken slumber.

Before I knew it, Greeny had run over and jumped with both feet, kicking the podgier one in the head and propelling both of them away from each other like two pole magnets. Greeny fell onto an old couple sitting at a nearby table, and the roadman hit his head on the bar counter, breaking three whiskey glasses and cutting his ear open. It looked a bit like two bouncy balls colliding with each other and then bouncing around a room, destroying everything they hit.

Ren's attacker, who was around six foot seven, reached into a small cross-body bag. Which meant he was about to pull out a knife. I knew it, I could just see it.

I was still holding a tequila shot glass in my hand, and before I knew it, I was hitting him over the head repetitively until it smashed and cracked, cutting his bald head.

This guy was so angry that it took me hitting him five times over the head with a glass cup for him to release Ren's throat.

After the fifth hit, he turned to me; I realised how in over my head I was now. He towered over me, looking down, his eyes red with rage, his neck and forearm muscles pumping full of adrenaline.

I took a deep breath and raised my hands to my chin, tensing my body, ready to take the onslaught of hands.

"Go on then, go on, let's fucking go, go on," I screamed, my voice quivering.

Out of the corner of my eye, James ran over with a full bottle of Pacifico beer and bottled the guy as hard as he possibly could.

Ren had just caught his breath and began to kick the guy on the ground repeatedly in the stomach.

"How do you like that, bitch! Not fun the other way round, is it!"

Greeny, who never had his shit together, was the most in control of his emotions, and he grabbed James and me by the collar and shouted at Ren.

"We need to go now."

We ran out of the pub down the road from Angel to a corner store in Shoreditch.

"WHAT THE FUCK WAS THAT ABOUT!" I yelled at James because I knew he was the one who instigated it.

"The guy was gonna sell us some shit weed," James said, panting. "But then…"

He takes some more deep breaths and squats down. "So I…"

A couple of deeper breaths.

"So I thought I'd fuck with him a bit; I put my name as Undercover Police Officer and my number as 999."

"So he hit me in the face; can you believe it?"

James rolled onto his back and began hysterically laughing.

I wanted to be mad, I did, but that kind of behaviour is quite brilliant. We all laughed, except Greeny, who actually seemed genuinely upset by the situation.

"We almost killed each other."

Everyone went silent, and the funny expressions on our faces melted into frowns.

"Greeny, give me two of those Valiums and a bump of coke. I'm going to see Amora; I need to balance out this adrenaline."

He did, and I began to walk through Shoreditch toward Shoreditch House.

So essentially, never sext.

"All right, Courtney, I need you to sign an NDA saying you

won't take any action if there are adverse effects. Read through and tick the boxes, then sign."

I pretended to look through the papers. "Carry on."

"Right, well I, um, well, I was a little..."

CHAPTER 14

"PUNCH DRUNK AND IT GOT ME THINKING."

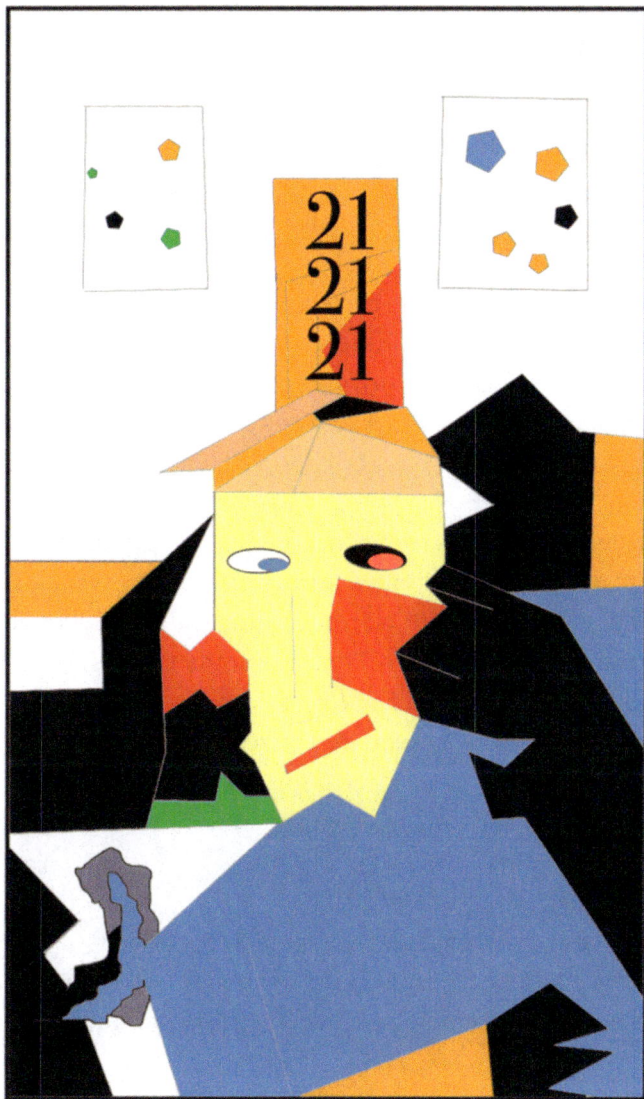

Now, there are a couple of reasons why fighting is not intelligent. Every man has a fantasy of what they are, what they would do in a physical altercation, and how they would go about it, and all it is is a fantasy.

Fantasy is not reality, and fighting in your head and fighting in real life are two completely separate things. Things I would learn.

I've watched much boxing, even trained when I was younger, and I'd been in a few street brawls with my friends and even got a black eye or two or three or four, but a fight—a real fight, one where you're fighting for your life—is different. Now let me explain why:

The substances I had taken with Greeny had entered my system; the Valium made me cool as a cucumber, and the cocaine sharp as a butter knife. The perfect mental state for a date.

I could see Amora standing outside Shoreditch House on a cobbled street, smoking a thin cigarette and checking her phone.

I waved to her from down the street, and she smiled and waved back. This was going to be good, my male ego whispered into my ear.

"You gonna have sex tonight, woohoo, you gonna have sex tonight, woohoo." I even skipped and tapped my feet in the air.

I had just got in a fight, won the fight, and now I was about to maybe potentially have sex. This was some tribal shit; I felt like a Viking, except instead of raping and pillaging, I was going to hopefully have some extremely consensual sex and pillage the bar for Picantes.

"'Ello, 'ello," I said whilst hugging and kissing Amora on the cheek.

"Hey, Court," she replied giddily.

"Shall we enter?" I opened the large door for her.

She looked at her phone again, which annoyed me because I was here now, and who else could be possibly more interesting than I?

She paused and looked up at me.

"We've just got to wait two minutes; my brother and his friend are coming too."

"Older or younger?"

"Older, but he's nice."

It is common knowledge that no older brother in the history of older brothers ever wants to see a guy with their younger sister, let alone a professional reprobate like myself.

It also meant that my chances of getting laid that night had decreased significantly, making me sad and slightly annoyed. I would have to now somehow walk a tightrope between being cool and chilled out for her brother, and then I would have to be charming and affectionate for Amora. Neither task fell into what my strengths were; however, I was up for the challenge. I did let out an unconscious "Fuck" under my breath.

To which she responded suspiciously with a "What" and cheeky grin because she knew exactly the kind of pressure that she was about to put me under.

"Oh, nothing, sorry," I replied, trying to look as relaxed as possible.

"It'll be fine," she said and then leaned in and kissed me.

That helped.

"Here he is now," she said, pointing over my shoulder to a black Range Rover with black tinted windows and black rims. I'm not Sherlock, but I know a drug dealer's car when I see one.

Rental plate, loud music, smoke coming out of the windows, aggressive speed, little to no indicating, and slightly lifted suspension.

But I decided to give him a chance; he could be a car enthusiast, or maybe he was an aspiring rapper.

I thought to myself, great, if he's a rapper, backstage passes; if he's a drug dealer, well, there were very few upsides to that, but perhaps it could raise my street credibility, which, as it stands, is less than zero.

The car pulled up, and I looked into the dark-tinted window. I could see my reflection in the window; I was grinning a little too much, so I toned down the smile to try to appear slightly nervous—which is a lie because I was invariably, definitely, without a doubt fucking nervous.

The window rolled down slow, real slow, inch by inch, centimetre by centimetre, revealing the brother's face and his friend.

To my dismay, they looked familiar.

They were covered in blood. Her brother, whom I could now see up close, shared many of the same features as Amora.

He was large, around six foot three, athletic, wearing a crossbody bag which definitely had a knife in it, and yes, his friend was smaller, podgier, Caucasian, and bleeding from the side of his head.

My shoulders slumped in disappointment, and I looked up to the sky, to God, and I genuinely said:

"Fuck you."

On later reflection, it sounded as though I was saying "fuck you" to her brother, whose face was already writhing with anger.

Amora was understandably confused by how mad her brother was with me and upset that he had been hurt.

She began to cry.

Her dearly beloved brother, whom she had talked about to me in such high regard so many times in so many ways, had been attacked by four of the biggest wrong'uns that London had to offer.

He wasn't even beaten up by anyone cool; he was beaten up by four two middle-class wankers, a toff and a semi-celebrity drug addict.

That would annoy me, too.

The Range Rover door opened forcefully, pushing me back to the kerb, and I assumed the boxing position—fists raised to my chin, legs bent, left arm ready to jab and keep the impending attack at bay for as long as I possibly could.

This was not the appropriate reaction; the appropriate reaction was to run and block Amora on everything later.

The thought crossed my mind that I was about to get stabbed. That is how severe this altercation was and how serious her brother was.

But I briefly remembered that I was a fencing champion when I was twelve, and by that logic, I supposed that I actually had a better chance of winning in a knife fight than a fistfight. The only issue was that I had no knife; I looked around, and there were no swords in the vicinity. By deducing what was around me, I concluded that boxing was going to have to do.

Whilst I was doing all of these equations in my head, deciding whether to run or to have a sword fight or box, Amora was yelling in the foreground whilst trying to hold her truly terrifying brother back.

The mix of her high-pitched screaming and his aggressive yelling came off as a mix of helpless violence.

I got a better look at her brother. He was mixed race, shaved head, bright green bloodshot eyes, a healed scar on his cheek and some newer open cuts on his forehead courtesy of my repeatedly beating him in the head with a small tequila glass.

This was it, my reckoning, but I reckoned that I had had about eight reckonings with God before, and he sent me back every time; there was comfort in that, but there was no doubt this one was going to hurt the most.

Bystanders started to watch on the street—about thirty wanky Soho House members watched—which was great because now I was going to be beaten to a pulp in front of some of the people I despised most on earth.

This could be worse than death.

I did hear one thing Amora said amongst the barrage of bystanders yelling to stop the punches.

"I might get my Soho House membership revoked if you kill him."

I thought to myself, it's very comforting that the bar is so low.

After all, being consistent in all aspects of life is key.

The podgy one got up in my face and said a bunch of threats along the lines of:

"You are not so big now, are you?"

To which I replied:

"No, but you are."

I laughed at my rather ill-timed joke, and he responded promptly and appropriately by punching me very hard and fast in my gut.

I knew it was coming, so I tensed and pretended to be winded strategically because I'd rather be beaten up by this podgy man than Amora's humongous brother.

I keeled over, holding my stomach, and the fat man said:

"Beg, bitch."

And then again:

"Beg, bitch."

Now, my male pride kicked in here. I'm no fighter, I know that. I'm not an angry person or even a person who would enjoy inflicting pain on another human.

But I'm not going to beg in front of her. So I stood up and simply said to him:

"No."

To which he then tried to punch me again, except this time I ducked, swung around him and pushed him, rugby style—honestly, a highlight moment in my very short fighting career.

His large podgy mass tripped on the sidewalk, and he tumbled to the ground. This was not my intention, and it meant his pride was on the line.

I had accidentally now gotten within punching range of Amora's terrifying brother by pivoting around her podgy friend and pushing him to the kerb.

I turned around to Amora's brother, whose eyes were lit ablaze with rage.

I gave him an awkward smile, the kind of smile that means

"time out" or "pause". This did not pause his advances.

Amora pleaded with me: "RUN! RUN!"

I should have run. Why didn't I run? I had Hinge; there were plenty more fish in the sea; surely this was not worth dying over.

But then what if it was? What if this was the beginning of a brilliant relationship, one where her brother and I could laugh out loud at Christmas and chat about how this was all a big misunderstanding one day whilst sipping eggnog by a fire? It was unlikely, sure, but not impossible.

If I can give you one piece of advice: if these kinds of thoughts ever pop up into your head in a fight, don't listen; that part of your brain is a prick, and get out pronto.

Now I think it was the drugs, honestly. Valium, cocaine and alcohol mixed together give you a god complex. Think about it: coke gives you synthetic confidence, Valium relieves all anxiety, and alcohol slows down your logic receptors.

So, somehow, I thought of myself as a negotiator in this situation, and all I had to do was calm this extremely volatile roadman from slitting my throat.

Sounded easy enough at the time.

So I tried:

"Hey, hey, this is all a big misunderstanding," I pleaded. "One day, we'll laugh about this," I said, smiling arrogantly. "Brothers?" I said with my arms out.

Now, to me, these were all very genuine attempts and advances at trying to reconcile.

But I can now see how, from his perspective, it could have come off as sarcasm or even satire.

However, on later reflection, he didn't strike me as the type of person to appreciate the nuances of satire or sarcasm.

My hands were in a negotiator position—not where they were supposed to be, by my chin.

He pushed Amora out of the way and, with all his might, swung his fist toward my cheek.

And then it happened—it went black.

I knew I felt the first punch because it scraped off some of the skin and flesh on my chin, which hurts if you were wondering.

Presumably, from a ring of sorts.

But the second one, the big right, the haymaker, I didn't see; I just didn't see it coming, and let me tell you, it's the punch you don't see that knocks you out.

Suddenly, I was floating in the sea, daydreaming about something stupid like whether I was going to buy a PS5 or the new Xbox (a serious point of contention). I was with Amora on holiday, maybe Spain or Greece, I couldn't tell; all I knew was it was somewhere hot. She was drinking some rosé fifty metres away on a beach. This pleased me because rosé is only meant to be drunk by the sea, and her understanding was going to be paramount to the longevity of our relationship. She was waving at me, signalling to come back.

Then she was yelling at me to come back, then I heard her screaming for me to come back, and then it was shrieking to come back.

I was surrounded by something dark in the water; underneath me, it swam underneath once, then twice.

I put my head under the water and looked down into the deep blue. Something was coming up for me, something big with teeth. So I began to swim as fast as I could toward the beach where Amora was.

I could feel the thing getting closer to my feet, touching the tips of my toes, almost biting.

But the beach, it seemed, was moving toward me too; it was a race—could the beach reach me, or would the thing eat me?

Then I came back.

A flashlight was in my right eye.

"Can you hear me?" an unfamiliar voice said.

I could hear, I could hear perfectly well, very well, in fact.

"I can hear; what do you want?"

I thought my mum was waking me up.

"Courtney, you're in an ambulance."

"Oh, right." I was remembering slowly but still wasn't sure if I was in the pub brawl or at home.

"Why may I ask?"

"Your left eye socket has been broken in a fight."

It all came flooding back.

Amora's brother had punched me, knocking my head against his Range Rover window, and then his podgy white mate had run over and stomped my head into a kerb four times, breaking the side of my cheek, eye socket and eyebrow.

I didn't care about that, though; I just wanted to know if Amora was with me.

"Amora!"

Some time went by, but then I heard a scared:

"I'm here, Courtney."

She was holding my hand.

Another person was with me, and I could tell by the tone it was a police officer.

"Hello, sir, do you have any information on who attacked you?"

I thought long and hard about this one; the decision I was about to make wasn't for Amora, it was for me and the rules I live by. If you do bad things, you have to come to terms with bad things happening to you. I may be a lot of things, but being a hypocrite is not one of them.

"I've got no idea, sir," I responded.

The officer let out a sigh. "Okay, sir."

Then he left, and it was me, Amora and a paramedic in an ambulance.

There was a lot of unsavoury tension in the room. I thought about it; it didn't have to be that way.

"I have to ask?" I said into the air because I couldn't see anything.

Amora was crying a lot but managed to get out a slow, sniffly

"What?".

I waited because timing is everything.

...

"How did the other guy look?"

The whimpering slowed.

"The same." She laughed a little through her tears.

Bingo.

"Not one graze? Nothing?" I asked again.

I pleaded jokingly, "Did I even throw a punch?"

"Shut up, Courtney." She laughed a little more, and we went to the hospital for surgery—not happy, but laughing and loving a little, at least.

"I'll take that as a no."

I learned that it's the punch you don't see that knocks you out.

The doctor came around. I closed my eyes, and he plunged the needle into my shoulder, putting the fluid into my system, then wiping the blood away and putting a plaster on it.

It was done; I could finally leave now. I got up to leave.

"Well, aren't you gonna tell me what happens?"

"Don't you have more clients?" I asked.

"For what you want this early, no; you and one other guy came in earlier and asked for the same thing."

"I probably know him."

"You probably do."

"He looked pretty weathered. He wasn't much of a talker, though."

Greeny, I thought to myself.

CHAPTER 15

Right, well, I was rolled from the ambulance into the hospital; it was a bumpy ride. One of the wheels didn't roll, which meant that the bed stopped and started a lot, creating an inconsistent jerk, followed by an appropriate English "sorry" from a female nurse whom I want to say was blonde. But my vision was blurry from the head injuries and from the medical nitrous oxide they were feeding me. They gave me nos because of a hospital-wide lack of painkillers and general anaesthetic. So I bumped along the hallways, occasionally getting a reactionary gasp from a passing mother who knew exactly what was going on. I think I even said "sorry" to a couple of people that had to look at my face. It was a very British affair: sorrys, free healthcare, packed hallways filled with the old, decrepit COVID-19 victims, and me, Amora, and my mum.

We were here again, in the bloody hospital, and at no fault of my own this time other than constantly choosing to mix with bad company. The days rolled on, and more police officers came to ask me, "Who has done it." I never told; Amora was worth not telling anyway, plus it was kind of like a self-inflicted punishment in a strange way. Just like don't play with fire because you might get burnt, the same logic applies to six-foot-five athletic-built road-men who drive Range Rovers and casually carry around hunting knives on a Wednesday.

I looked ugly. By the third day of surgery, my face looked ugly: my cheek drooped a little low, and my left eye didn't open as it used to. I would go back and forth between the mirror and the bed, high on codeine, very down. It was strange; one of my eyes was normal (dark blue), and the other was bruised, which meant the white was black, and my iris was red. The more I looked into the mirror, you got used to it; it was as though I saw myself for who I was really, for the first time. Completely ordinary right side and an evil goblin-looking left side. Two-faced.

This was not without benefit. The codeine, for one, was overprescribed as I lied about how much the eye hurt in an attempt to get free OxyContin. But the best thing about it was it was the first time I understood what it felt like to be perceived as a freak. Don't get me wrong, I think of myself as a kind of cool freak, but I realised I had given myself far too much credit. When you look like a freak, people treat you accordingly. At parties, ordinary people who would normally say hello either hugged me stayed away from me or were completely and utterly fascinated. They wanted to take pictures of the crimson red eye and stitches. I didn't mind the long stares or the people who stayed away; it was the pitiful hugs that get you.

They hug you like you're pathetic, a little puppy to be coddled, and that's not to say that I didn't want to be coddled, but Amora was doing a great job of that. To give you context of how bad this epidemic of longing, pitiful hugs got: some bitch—yes, I'm going to use the word, it's appropriate—some bitch named Rebecca, whom I had never met before in my life, hugged me for ten minutes, weeping because she claimed to know my pain. Rebecca lives in a mansion in the Cotswolds, and her daily struggle is trying to convince Papa's friends to buy her naked self-portraits.

News flash, Rebecca: they're buying them because you're naked in them, not because you're good at art.

I'll move on now to the most inconvenient thing about being beaten up everywhere.

There is a lot of weight that comes with being beaten up badly; the people feeling sorry for you thing is embarrassing. The actual pain of the head hurts. Taking too much codeine does not make you happy when you have to stop. The interior decor of the Royal London Hospital is not—well, it's not exactly The Standard (the restaurant/club that it is). But the worst fucking thing, the real fucking kick in the sack, was that my right hand was broken. I was so jacked up earlier in the night that I hadn't realised that I had broken my right hand smashing a tequila glass into that guy's head. It had completely cut my hand open, to the point where I had glass go all the way through the muscle, which meant it was in a sling.

So I was stuck in a hospital and couldn't type, bathe, eat, play video games, or use Hinge. But most importantly, I couldn't watch porn—well, I could, I just had to completely adjust to my left hand. This was not something that felt comfortable; it felt foreign. Then I thought about it a little more and decided that foreign was good. Then I missed variation, and having sex with a sewn-up lip and broken hand is far from a sexy ordeal, so that was kind of out of the question—well, from Amora's standpoint, that was. I didn't see the problem, which was in and of itself a problem. But just typing in something like "big booty" with your left hand onto a phone—it takes about three minutes longer than it would if you were using your right. Secondly, you then have to find a place to rest the phone because you can't hold it with your right; that involves a hospital chair, maybe some children's books to prop up the screen to eye level, which makes you feel like a scumbag. Then there's the clean-up, which, as a man, is literally a continuous low and pathetic moment that you now have to go through in the context of a hospital surrounded by dying people and old people named Gemma who have cancer. R.I.P. Gemma, you came into my hospital room that one time and pretended to care about boxing for me. In return, I listened to some boring story about your granddaughter in marketing. But you were mostly cool.

Anyway, now you know. If I have one piece of advice for you: if you're going to get into a fight, ball up your fist appropriately, and if you have feminine or dainty hands like me, use them for flipping the enemy off, not repeatedly punching them in the head. They will look and work better for that.

If you want a foreign experience, try your left hand.

"That's rough, can I have a look at the stitches."

I ignored him.

"Just to be clear, this is going to be on the government's system, right?" I said, pointing at my shoulder.

"Yeah, of course, I'm not an amateur."

The fact that he liked my stories scared me.

"You don't relate to any of these stories, do you?" I asked, now genuinely concerned for my health.

He shook his head whilst nodding. That's worrying.

"Okay, well, after I left the hospital, I went to visit.

CHAPTER 16

JAMES IN THE COUNTRYSIDE

He was still confined to his country house where his mother had sheltered him, too, after all we had gone through in the last couple of months. His mother explained that he would be cut out of the family will if he ever came to London before getting his master's in New York. I didn't like the bitch, but it was probably a good call. So James asked Greeny and me to come up to his home for his last weekend before being banished to the land of the free, never to be seen again until he had some kind of academic clout.

So Greeny and I bumped the northwestern rail, hiding in a small toilet cabinet for two hours, waiting to arrive at a small town called Bucks. The place was full of aristocrats with no money, large estates, awful old English empire attitudes, pheasant shooting ranges and a lot of blonde women. I don't like blonde women, so that displeased me. It's the type of place David Cameron and Boris Johnson go for Christmas, if you get my drift.

Upon arrival, we went out immediately—I mean, Greeny and I didn't even drop our bags inside; we just put them on the doorstep of what I could only make out as a large estate in the dark and hit the town with James.

Upon waking up inside the estate the next day, I could see James standing in the doorway of his parents' great estate in his boxers, smoking a cigarette in one hand and holding a vape in the other. A posh-looking and rather embarrassed naked blonde girl collected her clothes from behind him. Greeny walked over and sat on the stairs in the doorway, fiddling with a Rubik's cube.

"You all right, sober boy?" James says half-jokingly, knowing he defeated my will again last night.

"Better than you, I assume."

James looks over his shoulder at the blonde and then back at me with a smile.

"You tell me."

We both laugh at the expense of the girl.

"Saturday roast?"

"You read my mind," Greeny chimes in.

The blonde kisses James on the cheek and says something about meeting her parents, to which James replies:

"Sure."

She looked up at my still blackened eye, grimaced slightly, looked at James in a way that insinuated a realisation, and then shrugged—probably saying in her mind, "It is what it is"—and scurried away down the country road probably to go back to her own large estate.

James walked down the stairs, and we followed.

The estate was massive; it had all of James's ancestors on the walls—the great blah blah blah of blah blah, who gives a fuck—painted on every wall in every hall. The ceilings were monumental; if you wanted to, you could fit a giraffe in the main hall. The furniture was old English leather, green and maroon, with gold and old wood. It was beautiful and grand and large. But it was lonely; James was the only one here.

At least in London, you're never five feet away from someone, whether that be a drunk, a crackhead, a guy grabbing a takeaway, someone smoking a cigarette—the list goes on—but you're not alone. Despite its beauty, the estate was a glorified golden cage.

We hovered around James's island in what I would assume would have been the servants' kitchen some time long ago for a Saturday roast. A Saturday roast is like a Sunday roast, except you make it yourself, and if you don't have any ingredients that would typically be in a Sunday roast, that makes no difference at all. A Saturday roast is not about roasted meat, potatoes, stuffing, Yorkshire puddings, or even the bloody gravy—although it is better if you do have those things.

A Saturday roast is about having someone debrief you on what you did or didn't do to mitigate any future hangover trauma. There are a couple of themes to a Saturday roast: number one, you need an island in your kitchen. I'm only joking, but I thought this was a good segue into a quick observation about kitchen islands.

Quick interlude about why the kitchen island is an absolute necessity (and no, I don't have one—I know they're expensive):

1. When you enter a party, you need a point of direction. The sofa is too relaxed, too personal; you may have to enter into a conversation you don't want to, and then you're trapped for at least thirty minutes. The island, on the other hand, offers a place to put your drinks, assess the room, the exits, where your friends are, where they aren't, the girls, the boys, the drugs and the thugs. All can be assessed safely in a casual way from the island.

2. Chatting around an island is not a commitment; it's a gesture. "Hi, I'm Courtney," I say on one side of the island. We look at one another, and the other person can decide to do a quick French exit, or they can stick around and get chatting.

3. They usually have stools and not chairs. There is something about bending down and pulling out a chair at a table that feels like you're going to be there for a while, whereas a stool is very different. A stool is higher; it gives you a vantage point in terms of sight. They also swivel, allowing you to enter different conversations whenever you want.

4. Finally, an island is taller than a table; this allows for better drink pouring, casual snack grabbing, and less awful physical activity, which is bending down.

Segue closed—

A Saturday roast is essentially a breakdown of where you're at, what you've done, and all things current to twenty-one-year-old men and women.

I sit comfortably on a pink felt stool and observe the kitchen; it reeks of old money. The chairs look nice aesthetically but do not fulfil a chair's basic purpose of being comfortable.

Looking around, it's clear James's family likes to spend.

The room is amuck with David Hockneys—not the originals but expensive prints—and other artists from the modernism movement. There are Oxford dictionaries and various other books and articles that give off the appearance of an academic, intelligent and civilised household.

Which is ironic, as they are none of those things. James is grinning from ear to ear, still in his briefs, his cigarette now burning to its butt, ash going in between the wooden floorboards—not a care in the world. Greeny, on the other hand, still focuses intensely on the Rubik's cube.

Greeny seems to be quite upset about the lack of roast ingredients, which he emits out of his mouth and into the air.

"I know your mum is never home, your dad's a cunt, and you never buy any shopping, but for God's sake, buy some fucking food."

James was transfixed on the more important task of trying to make us French toast. His frustration with this belittling task grew with the spatula flip.

"You know we're going to order food, Greeny," I chime in, knowing full well the direction that this entire scenario was headed.

"And beer—a non-alcoholic beer, that is, of course." They both sigh in disappointment; I understand.

"Can you even order a Sunday roast on Saturday?"

"We are in Bucks; I feel like there should be some kind of delivery service around here," James says in an attempt to imitate something Greeny said a while back but subsequently insulting his privilege, too.

"So the classic Saturday roast, McDonald's it is?" Greeny says, unamused at this predictable outcome.

We agree.

"This one's on you, Court," Greeny laughs, knowing neither of us has any money.

"I pay for mine," I respond, agitated by the truth of the comment.

"All right, pipe down, sober boy," James says, scrolling through his phone and looking for food delivery apps.

"JUST EAT!" James shouts at his phone.

"Just eat what?" I reply.

"No, JUST EAT."

"What?"

"NO, JUST EAT."

"JUST EAT WHAT? YOU HAVE NO FOOD IN THE HOUSE!"

I shout and jump out of my chair. James jumps out of his.

We square off.

Greeny reminds me that Just Eat is a food delivery app. I sit back down.

James orders the usual: five chicken selects, five large fries, three Big Macs, and three Coca-Colas.

There are no Uber Eats or Deliveroo in the English countryside.

"Carry on."

I was starting to like this doctor, even if he was a bit of a reprobate himself.

"I asked the room."

CHAPTER 17

"WHO WANTS TO DEBRIEF?"

I say whilst dipping a Chicken Select in some barbecue sauce.

Greeny tosses the Rubik's Cube onto one of the pieces of useless leather furniture after he realises that he cannot complete it.

"I'll do it." He stands and walks in a circle with his hands behind his back, like a professor, a deep-thought analyser, a man who has something to say and is about to deliver it well.

"Well, my friends, last night began with the coke hunt." James and I nod in agreement.

"Courtney, do you care to give your thesis on the coke hunt?" James asks.

I will, except I'll explain it to you instead of how it was told, in case anyone is particularly offended by how un-politically correct the true story is. A coke hunt is exactly what it sounds like—you are hunting for cocaine.

"But hunting for cocaine is so easy these days; all you have to do is message them on WhatsApp, and they'll be there in thirty minutes," I hear you degenerates and reprobates say.

I know it's what you're thinking.

No, this is about hunting for cocaine the good old-fashioned way, the eighties way—a way that involves humiliation, suffering, awkward encounters and even the occasional slap.

One does not choose the cocaine hunt; the cocaine hunt chooses you. In Bucks, there are three pubs; in one of those three pubs, there is a cocaine guy—you have to find him. But you don't leave the house—or, in this case, the mansion—with the intention of wanting cocaine.

No, it usually happens around the fifth point; the conversation will die down a bit. You'll look at one another, and one of you will float the idea. In terms of our night, James said:

"I wish we had some bag."

All of our ears sprang up—what an idea, a solution, the way to make this dreary night not so dreary.

The pub we were in was very quiet, sleepy and on the side of a hill surrounded by beautiful old windmills. The occupants in the pub were composed of a family, one drunk, three nervous teenagers and a couple on a date.

Greeny and I looked through our phones and did the first thing you must do to avoid the following events in this story:

Text your London dealers.

Firstly, you send out some feelers like:

"Will you deliver to Bucks?" To which they will inevitably reply, "No." Then, you will follow it up by asking, "Do you know any dealers in Bucks?" They will not reply to that either.

Once you realise that you have no power out in these rolling country hills and the rules of London do not apply, it's James's turn to begin the hunt.

James texts anyone in the area that he may or may not know if they happen to know any drug dealers.

You ease them into this and keep the text brief. A simple text says:

"Do you know any drug dealers in the area? Me and my buddies want to smoke some weed."

None of us smoke weed, but people are so judgemental these days. In our case, that didn't work; we got one weed dealer to answer the phone, but James scared him off by demanding that he find us a cocaine dealer immediately.

I looked around the pub and decided that the drunk was our best bet; now, we just needed to decide which one of us was going to do it.

I strategically offered to go, knowing that if he didn't have coke, the next best people were the teenagers, and asking them would be far more mortifying than asking the drunk.

So I swaggered over, a little too confident, a little too drunk, my head down, looking at the old varnished wooden plank floor before arriving at my destination next to him at the quiet bar.

"You all right, mate?" I said in a friendly manner.

"WHAT!" the drunk replied. I could see the wrinkles in his puffy face, hard white skin and red eyes.

"I said, how are you doing?"

He responded with some inaudible drunk sentence, but I understood by the general tone and direction of the syllables that he meant:

"Bloody Southerner."

I took a step back from him and thought about it; I watched him swaying and staring at his empty glass.

"WOULD YOU LIKE A PINT?" I asked loudly.

He perked up; I saw that artificial light in his eyes, but it didn't deter me.

"Yes, lad, aye lad, I'd love one." His voice rumbled, I'm assuming from too many nights in this pub and long-term cigarette smoking.

"All right, well, if you can tell me where I can get some bag, my brown-haired friend over there will get you as many pints as your heart desires," I said, pointing over to James, who looked back at me confused.

"BAG!" he yelled. "WHAT'S BAG?!"

The pub went silent for a second but then resumed its sleepy, slow pace.

"Nose candy, toot, bugle, marching powder, the Peruvian, the Bolivian, the Colombian white stuff?" I said, whispering but making the universal gesture of sliding my finger under my nose.

"WHAT?" he said again.

I rolled my eyes and internally gave up.

"DO YOU KNOW WHERE I CAN BUY SOME FUCKING COCAINE?"

He looked at me and said, "No."

"Well, no pints for you then," I said, walking back to the table.

We had a team talk with the guys about who and how we were going to move forward effectively and efficiently. Me being the poorest of the trio meant that I had to affirm my position in the group by taking risks for the group. I had taken the risk, the first step; now it was Greeny's go. Greeny being very anti-social meant that he had a very small chance of getting anyone in this lovely countryside pub to tell him their secret. But the thing about Greeny was he was an addict. Sure, James and I were bad, there was no doubt about it; we had issues we were avoiding, but Greeny's life was constant—he never felt a hangover because he was never not high.

If there was one thing about Greeny that you could rely on, it was that he was not going to give up the hunt.

"Greeny, you're up next, buddy," James said confidently, knowing that in the event of us actually finding any drugs, he would most likely be the one paying for them. Greeny looked around and analysed the room; an ultra-focus set in. He was looking for clues; the drunk was just a drunk—well, if you drink as much as that guy drinks, you might as well be doing drugs—but anyhow, he was of no use to us.

The couple were young, in their early thirties, potential residents of this area for sure. They were relaxed in this environment; it clearly wasn't their first time eating here, and it wasn't going to be their last. The family was a no-go; they were past the threshold for the kind of activities that we wanted to get up to—this wasn't their game anymore, and even if it was, they wouldn't want anyone to know.

Greeny's eyes closed in on the teenagers; they were something teen years old, probably at the weed-smoking phase of their life, the kind of stage where all you do is talk about girls and not to them. They would look at us like we were gods of some order, completely ignorant, in awe of how we dressed and our nonchalant behaviour. Unaware of what they were looking at, confused by tattoos, an attitude and somewhat of a unique fashion sense. But they were civilians; it was best to leave them alone. I didn't want to bring them down to our level yet—it best to let them get here by themselves or avoid the whole ordeal altogether.

Just like a soldier making a decision and knowing he has to stick to it, Greeny downed his pint and walked over to the couple. His entire demeanour changed; his anxiety was not there. He walked confidently; he didn't have his constant deep-thought face on; instead, his face was smiling, cocky even. He looked the kind of guy who could walk into any room and make friends. James and I were taken aback—what were we witnessing? Was it possible that Greeny, the worst of us all, was just holding back all the time? We watched from our table, clutching our pints in anticipation as he began to schmooze the couple.

I couldn't tell what he was saying, but his hand gestures and mouth movements gave me the impression that the conversation went a little like this:

"Hi there, guys. Sorry to bother you both on this fine evening. My friends and I are new to this town and about to celebrate with a friend who lives in the area. He is a bit of a—well, let's just say he's a fun guy who likes to have a fun time…. Now, I know it's a big ask, but would you happen to know any drug dealers in the area?"

The man looked at him and then laughed. I could faintly hear his accent—he was an Aussie.

Bingo, we had hit the jackpot.

The guy gave Greeny some instructions, something along the lines of down the street and on your right.

Greeny responded with a big smile and wished them the best for the night.

He then walked back, slumped into his chair and turned directly back into the anti-social, slightly moody Greeny James and I knew.

"Well?" we both asked.

"Apparently, there's a bald old Chinese man who sells coke down the street. He sits in a dingy restaurant with misty windows, and it's called 'Fu King Chinese.'"

"Fuck yeah, this night, this journey wasn't complete after all; there is still hope," I let out.

James downed his pint, and we all put on our jackets and walked to the door, saluting the Aussie as we walked out and him saluting us back.

Tonight was going to be an adventure; the boys were taking over a small town tonight, and with the cold wind on our back, we made our way down the quiet streets of Bucks toward the glowing yellow restaurant in the distance. Rain began to pour, so we jogged toward it; the hunt for the artificial light had begun.

We approached the restaurant, and faint Chinese music chimed out of it, but there were no conversations, no customers. The only thing that would have alluded to it being open was the light that shone dimly out. James hit his vape and blew it in the air; it would have looked cool, but he started to cough profusely, which led to Greeny and me overflowing with laughter. Once the laughing stopped, we all stretched and clicked our necks and knuckles.

I went in first, then Greeny, then James; a doorbell rang as we walked in. The inside of the restaurant was filthy and bare in a way that couldn't be cleaned away. The once-white walls were cigarette-stained to yellow, and the corners of the room had collected a cloud of thick black dust that had been left there too long to now be cleaned away. Inside were two tables, one on the left and the other on the right. We could not see a bald Chinese man; however, one old lady was sitting at the left table facing the wall, drinking sake and staring into nothingness. She looked like she was a part of the furniture. On the right was an empty table with three stools and some chopsticks laid out on some thin, cheap-looking napkins. At the back was an empty bar with no one behind it except for one picture of a city in China, maybe Beijing or Shanghai. We sat at the table on the right.

Greeny and I had done our part, and now it was James's turn. After taking off his jacket and carefully placing it on the back of his stool, he walked toward the bar. The restaurant was so quiet that no matter what he said, Greeny and I would be able to hear it.

"Helllooooo," James said to a wall. No answer.

"Helllllooooooooo," he said once again with no answer. By the third time, he raised his voice a little.

"HELLO, IS ANYONE THERE?"

A bald and very old Chinese man walked out. Greeny and I chuckled in excitement at the fact that we were not the ones who were going to have to have this interaction.

James put his elbow on the table and leaned in over the counter to whisper.

"Do you sell cocaine here?"

The man leaned backwards and squinted at James; he looked angry for a second and then smiled.

His smile revealed a set of yellow and black teeth. The man nodded.

"How much?" James asked, pulling out a wad of cash.

The man called out in Chinese for another, and an identical copy of the bald man walked out.

They were twins.

They spoke in Chinese, and then both smiled at one another again.

"Take a seat; we'll be right with you," one of the twins said.

"All right, fine, but don't take too long; I've got places to be," James retorted in his dismissive, entitled tone and pointed at his Rolex watch, tapping the dial.

"Anything to drink whilst you wait?"

James looked around the room and then at the zoned-out lady.

"I'll have whatever she's having."

Both men walked behind a wall to prepare the necessary things.

All of us looked at one another with pride; we had done it— against all odds, we had beaten this little town and the challenges that had come with it.

The man brought the sake plus three small serving glasses, and the other twin brought over three large glasses with ice and lemons.

We all raised a glass to one another and swallowed the hot sake.

Just at the height of our excitement, the purity of our joy, the feeling of exhilaration, the man came over with three glass bottles of Coke.

The great wall of reality came crashing down, and all of our faces dropped in mutual disappointment.

The Chinese men stood behind the counter, raising their eyebrows in amusement. The lady, who we thought was too drunk to even understand where she was, let alone understand what we were saying, started to burst out in laughter.

They were laughing at us—at James's entitled attitude, how drunk we were, the whole charade—they thought we were a joke.

But the funny thing is, we were a joke.

Upon this realisation, a beautiful thing happened.

Greeny began to chuckle, then laugh along with the people in the restaurant. I couldn't help but laugh too.

Then after, even James entertained the idea.

"Bloody fucking Aussie," he let out. "Bloody FUCKING AUSSIE," he laughed.

We had been duped, and everyone was in on the joke except for us. I bet that Aussie and his date were crying with laughter.

Well, at least now, we were too.

It was so funny that we sat there laughing all night until the restaurant closed, sipping sake with the lady and the old men, reminiscing on the good, the bad and the ugly of twenty twenty-one.

The Aussies are a rowdy bunch of brilliant criminals.

"Well, what did you do after that?"

A man in overalls came into the room and grabbed a large metal keg from behind me.

"Well, I went out again in London and fucked up badly, like losing my job badly. The bad where you..."

CHAPTER 18

"HIT THE WALL"

It was clear to me as I lay squeezed into the corner of my loft bed, face squished against the cold wall—I had fucked it. I could feel the warmth on my back, and I could smell the sour alcohol remnants of champagne escaping my body from both me and what looked like a six-foot-three Russian lady who was spooning my back ferociously. I am not upset about the Russian lady or even about being the little spoon; sex is sex, and that's another notch on the old sex wall crossed off. It is three p.m., which means I have missed three meetings with my creative director, and I am going to potentially have to come to terms with the fact that I may be a sex addict. That is worrying, but as far as addictions go, honestly, it's not so bad.

I climb out of bed, and my feet crunch on the ground—not like the crisp crunch of food or some plastic, no, my feet have just put all their weight onto the surprisingly familiar feeling of broken glass mixed with carpet. I am now awake.

"FUCK!"

The Russian girl murmurs something along the lines of "Come back to bed."

I look back and decide that is not a good idea, for now anyway. The next thing is finding my phone to deal with the incoming onslaught of inevitable urgent emails, missed calls, angry texts and social media notifications.

I pick up the iPhone, which is sticky from what appears to be dry champagne. I look from left to right in an attempt to find water or wipes or something to wipe it down. Nothing in sight—got to use spit.

"Huck, spu…"

You've got to do what you've got to do. I spit on the phone and wipe it down to see my notifications.

Thirteen missed calls from Naomi, six texts all saying "Where are you?", "Are you on a bender?" "I cannot put up with this for much longer." You get the drift.

Moving on to Instagram notifications:

@Sydney221; 2 a.m.: "Courtney, it's two a.m. on a Sunday, for fuck's sake." Ouch.

@Charlottesnothere; 3 a.m.: "You only message me when you're drunk." True.

@Milliesnails; 4 a.m.: "This is my business account." Honestly, I'm sure my drunk self had his reasons.

@Greeneybean; 5 a.m.: "Dude, I don't have a coke number. It's fucking Monday morning." That is a bit harsh coming from a drug addict.

@Beatricelewin; 6 a.m.: "Courtney, I'm seeing someone." He didn't have to know.

@kristinashevkov; 6:30 a.m.: "My Uber is outside." That explains the situation. "Fuck?"

Now, to look at the real kicker, the work email. creativedirector@imaginethat.co.uk

URGENT: You have missed three creative reviews today.

Courtney, I hope this finds you well, but we regret to inform you that due to your absence from work, we are going to have to ask you to leave the company. I think you're a good creative, and perhaps I am to blame for taking you on this young, but people in the office have noticed that you seem hungover all the time, and I can't help but think that's the reason you aren't in today. It's been a pleasure having you here, and I wish you luck in any future endeavours.

Regards,

Lucie, ECD.

"Fuckidy, fuck fuck."

"Knock, knock." It's my mum.

"What?" I say, trying my best to sound alive.

"Naomi is here."

"Oh, for fuck's sake."

This is one of those moments when you realise it's over. It was always going to be, but this was it—the final straw. I could hear her footsteps and a loud sigh as she walked closer to the door. I knew what was coming; the email had already certified it, now was the final blow, the headshot, at my lowest, my room in shambles, lines of cocaine on a piece of broken mirror that was highlighted by the light coming in from where the blind was slightly ajar, reflecting what I've done in little broken shards of light all over the room. Two bottles of empty Taittinger on the floor, cigarettes stubbed out on my sofa. This is what failing looked like. Luckily, though, I did catch a glimpse of myself in the mirror, and my hair was perfectly slicked back. Have you ever woken up with the perfect mix of bed head to slick shape? It's picture-worthy. The biggest tragedy in this situation was that I would have to take a shower, which would ruin it—but the losing a job part wasn't great either.

"Courtney," a low-pitched, disappointed American voice said from my open door.

"Yeah, mate," I replied, pursing my lips and squinting my eyes in a way that expressed that I, too, was not ecstatic about my current circumstances.

"I hoped that you had fallen off your bike or something other than this bullshit."

I raised my arm, showing her a grazed elbow with a forced smile—it turns out I had indeed fallen off my bike on the way to the pub last night.

The room went silent; her animosity for me was growing.

"Well, I'm going to have to find a new copywriter."

I had nothing to say; how could I? This was bad, even by my standards.

The only thing that appropriately expressed how I felt about this situation was a long, extended and, quite frankly, defeat.

"Fuckkkkk."

She wished me luck and left the room. My mum peeked into the room, paused, shook her head and closed the door.

God, what I've put that woman through.

Just when I thought it couldn't get any worse, the Russian girl muttered, still half asleep in her bed and with a thick Russian accent.

"You are fucked. Teehee."

I twisted my rigid, bruised, hungover body around and told her with calm, serene rage—the kind of rage that isn't intended to scare. It intends to harm.

"Get the fuck out of my house."

She did so quickly, and I sat there. Everything went opaque; everything went clear; everything got real. I saw my future for the first time, and it was bleak. No more warm feelings of home comfort, no more excuses, no more 'it's time to change', 'it's not me, it's them'—everything lost its depth. I had exceeded everyone's expectations of what I was incapable of. There were no expectations left, just me. A huge relief fell over my shoulders; something dark that seemed to always be in the same room as I had left. It had walked out, completing its task and moving on to the next lost individual willing to indulge in self-loathing and pitiful excuses to not do what you know needs doing. I thought back to what Soll said to me a year ago now.

"Your lowest low is the first high."

But if that's true, then maybe it's also true that before you reach your highest high, you have to have your lowest low.

I cleaned up my room, drank a gallon of water, hoovered up the broken glass, swore to my mum I would replace the champagne, ate some fruit, did two hundred push-ups—not in a row, of course—and checked Instagram.

Amongst the rubbish, the social climbing, the fake friendly comments, gym bro toxic masculinity quotes and the pictures of half-naked OnlyFans girls, I saw someone peeking their positive little bald head out—a pale, red, skin-coloured muscular ball of hope shimmering, talking into a microphone. I click the link. "This month is Sober October, and if you're hungover, it's the time to start over," blah blah blah, something about a runner's high—Joe Rogan.

I'd read about it. I'd heard the stories of boredom for a month. I'd seen friends disappear from friend groups; conversations got more awkward, smokers turned to chain smokers, espressos consumed at ungodly hours and motivational videos on Instagram. But I couldn't continue this; I would have one last hurrah before twenty-twenty-two with Greeny, and then I'd start a new one.

Lesson: The unlubricated penis of life cums both hard, fast and all at once.

CHAPTER 19

The club was just a walk away.

"For whom we are seeing, you should turn your Snap Maps off," Greeny instructed.

"That sounds bad."

When we arrived, I noticed only one window in the whole building had light emitting from it—the third floor.

A bouncer opened a door for us immediately, having seen us at the club now twice a week for the last five years. The club is well-designed; it has three floors. The bottom is a club, the top is like the second, and the second has zebra-striped floors, velvet maroon seats, low-lit lamps, a marble bar, and everything else is blurry because I have rarely ever been there sober. The club is either packed to the brim or empty, and there is no in-between.

Now, under normal circumstances, when you go to a private club that is empty, you'd leave. I would have thought that was dodgy, but once again, cocaine, ketamine, Valium and alcohol all have a way of making things seem different.

"Hello, boys," a high-pitched, scary voice said from inside.

I paused and gave Greeny a look that said, "I ain't going."

The camp voice said again:

"Boys, we know you're there." Another voice laughed from inside.

"I count two," I whisper to Greeny.

He swallowed nervously.

I look at Greeny and shake my head. This is the moment when we could turn back—a moment when we rarely do but when we could.

We powered on, putting on our best confident smiles whilst checking each other's noses for white residue, and walked into the sitting room.

Two suspiciously masculine women sat at the table looking up at us, their posture perfectly upright, practised even, their make-up thick, white and overdone. They were wearing wigs, heavy black eyeliner, and bright red lipstick; they looked ridiculously scary. One of the heavier-set ladies looked like a bloke dressed as a woman; the other also looked like a man dressed as a woman.

As we walked from the door to the far side of the room, I faintly heard Greeny mutter under his breath.

"Fuck."

The tone and octave of this singular word instructed me we were in for a ride that one did not wish to be in for. A Spanish barman I had conversed with on multiple occasions avoided eye contact with me as he shook a cocktail shaker, making it very evident that either he thought I didn't want him to know I was here or that he didn't want to know I was here.

The two—let's just call them ladies for now—stood up to greet us. Greeny is not small, and I was about six foot, but when these ladies embraced us, I felt small; my head was on the big blonde one's bosom, and Greeny's head was under.

One of them hugged me, whilst the other hugged Greeny. Despite the drugs and alcohol, my brain was making the connection slowly, if ever, but it was making the connection—these were no ladies, they were transvestites, which was fine, absolutely fine, more than fine. However, what wasn't fine was what agreement I had seemingly walked into without knowing what Greeny and these lovely ladies had agreed to before we entered.

From the embrace, it was clear that the arrangement was not one of the platonic kind. A hug that goes on for about one minute is never a good sign.

We sat, and the courting ritual that I usually bestowed upon women was now being bestowed upon me.

We were about to play chess, and the loser was going to have to give the other a blowjob.

My move.

"So, how do you guys know Greeny then?"

The transvestites looked at one another in a way that insinuated they had sex without overtly saying that sex had happened.

A couple of seconds went by, and I noticed from the silence that neither Greeny nor the transvestites were sure of whether this was a conversation they were allowed to have out loud.

I reassured them.

"Hey, I'm liberal, I won't judge." I was lying.

A couple more awkward seconds went by, and they were now on the defensive. Perhaps I could leverage this situation to get free drinks and then slink off to a girl's house later on.

"A gentleman never tells," the smaller, slightly less busty transvestite laughed aloud.

Greeny looked up at me, embarrassed. I understood then and there that this was not a situation he wanted to be spoken out loud. No need to push; I'm no saint.

"So what are you boys looking to do tonight?" the larger, more busty transvestite laughed.

"Drink," Greeny responded cheekily and quickly.

"Drink, we can do." The large transvestite snapped his fingers, and without a word, the Spanish barman began to make ten espresso martinis.

"We are testing alcohol tonight. Would you like to try?"

"Does a tiger change its stripes?" Greeny said, energised and alluding to previous experiences he had had.

A tray of drinks was put down by the Spanish man.

"You all right, mate?" I said to break the tension and address the fact that I knew the barman—both for the safety of having a witness there to make sure no dodgy movements were made and to clearly show and express my innocence.

He looked up at me and smiled, but his eyes said something else; they said you need to leave, you need to get out, this is not a safe place. His eyes said I've seen things happen here that you don't want to know about; if you don't leave now, you'll leave here different. I should have listened to those eyes.

There are two ways to approach a sexually precarious situation. The first is with a sober, healthy mindset—the kind of headspace when you go into the situation with the hope and belief that whatever experiences you will encounter that night, for good or bad, will be formative. The other is and will always be, fuck it, why not?

I chose fuck it, why not; I've been inside for two years, so why not experiment. As the night progressed, Greeny drank two, and I drank two, and they ordered more and more and more.

They just sipped their drinks, watching us consume their alcohol—lambs to the slaughter.

Greeny and I were almost in what I would describe as an utterly paralytic state when they hit us with what they wanted.

The big one snapped his fingers again, this time twice and in the air.

The Spanish barman, who was cleaning glasses, put down what he was doing, dimmed the lights in the room and walked out, closing the door behind him. I looked up from my slumber.

"Would either of you boys like a blowjob?"

I spat out my drink onto my white T-shirt; well, I say spat, I essentially dribbled my drink onto my now not even particularly white shirt.

"I'm sorry?" I said, more astonished at their honesty than anything else.

I don't know why I reacted that way; I knew this was exactly what they wanted from us from the moment I walked in.

Greeny looked at me, but this time, he looked different; he had brought me here knowing this was the trade—free fucking drinks for a blowjob.

Not even Soll nor James would indulge in this. But they had left me here; it wasn't fun anymore; I couldn't romanticise this.

The seconds ticked and tocked by as they awaited my response, and I thought and thought.

On the one hand, I would essentially be getting a blowjob from two large men dressed as women. If I indulged in this, perhaps I would have to question certain aspects of my sexuality.

Or worse than that.

What if I enjoyed it so much that I became a homosexual convert? But then, at the same time, saying no to head is very gay.

If we are using gay as a derogatory term.

Considering the above internal monologue, I feel I'm allowed to do it. I think I may be overthinking this.

"Let me clean my shirt quickly," I said.

The bigger one clicked his fingers twice again, and the door opened.

I looked at Greeny, and he looked back at me. He blinked one last time slowly; it was a slow blink, but I knew it meant goodbye.

I turned around and began to walk. The room was spinning, but I knew if I could get out of this building, I could live with myself; there was still time to change, to be something better in the future.

I got to the door and out of their sight.

The barman was waiting at the door just out of sight of the two old men. He grabbed my arm on the way out; I flinched slowly and fell loudly.

"Do you need any help?" the more petite old man shouted from inside the dark room.

The barman said back inside, "All good."

He pointed down the stairs toward an open door.

I stumbled down the stairs, hitting the left and right bannisters and zig-zagging downward until I got to the door. I looked up to see if Greeny was following, but he wasn't.

I pushed the exit door open and was immediately hit by the cold December frosty air.

It was windy and hailing, but I could see the local corner store about one hundred metres away from me, glowing, blurry—a beacon of hope.

I pushed onward through the frosty air that tried with all its might to push me back.

Every twenty metres, I looked up at the one window with light coming out of it—the one room with Greeny. I walked further and further away, looking back to see if that light was still on.

I got twenty metres away, and I looked up, and one of the men was looking out the window; I was hidden in December darkness.

The further I got away, the more I knew that, at some point, that light was going to go out, and when it did, Greeny was beyond the point of saving.

The figure in the window walked out of sight, and I ran from the convenience store across the road to a corner; I peeked around one last time to see if Greeny was behind me.

He wasn't there, the lights were out, and I headed home to watch *Bridgerton*.

CHAPTER 20

"THE END OF A JOB"

It is never a good thing; your subconscious plays tricks on you, negative thoughts start to slowly seep into your daily routine, and you make rash choices.

It all started with a call from Greeny on a Wednesday night—the Wednesday part is key because when you decide to go out midweek, you know what you're in for; it is almost always not coming from a place of reason. Greeny had called telling me there was a party at some shit club in Grove. When I got to his flat in Westbourne Grove, there was no party, but what there was lots of was four grams of ketamine and three grams of cocaine that Greeny had bought using the money he earned playing a set at Elizabeth's.

A sober Courtney, a thinking Courtney, a Courtney with a job would have walked into that room and turned around immediately, understanding that the situation would not end positively. I knew this night was going to hell.

Greeny and I had become accustomed to getting old weird men and women to buy us drinks—kind of like sugar daddies and mummies except for no sexual favours. I'm not proud of that; in fact, to a certain capacity, it is a very demeaning endeavour, but Greeny and I can't afford twenty-pound Picantes, and that is that.

I walked into his flat, which was on a council estate in Westbourne Grove, and he was already a mess; his flat consisted of five rooms: two bedrooms, one bathroom and one toilet. Greeny, like most twenty-year-old musicians, is a bum; he does just enough DJ gigs to keep his drug habit afloat whilst paying for rent. There are moulding bowls of pot noodles scattered amongst the room and empty cans of K cider crushed and overflowing out of a bin next to a small TV with Netflix playing on it in the background. His flat smells faintly of garlic. The garlic smell wasn't overpowering. It smelt more like he was trying to hide it. I wish he hadn't done that. Hiding it was worse; he should have just acknowledged the fact that his flat was a smelly dump with confidence, and we could have gotten on with the whole degenerate thing. But no, Greeny ignored the giant garlic-smelling elephant in the room and asked in his low-pitched, slightly stupid voice:

"Want a line?"

I did want a line.

"Anything to block my nose would be appreciated."

"Huh?" Greeny replied, stupefied.

I snort.

"So when's the party?"

"Oh, I got the date wrong—it's next week."

I realised that I should have asked that question before doing the cocaine, but once the desired cocaine effect had kicked in, I did not need silly thoughts like making good decisions and what I had to do the next day. These were things that were irrelevant, unnecessary, selfish thoughts.

"Well, what are we going to fucking do, Greeny?"

Greeny said nothing and looked down at his pile of drugs as though they had and would always be the answer to my question.

So we sat, smoked cigarettes, and Greeny talked about himself, never saying anything remotely interesting.

He just talked on and on about his art. Most artists have a way of making everything about themselves, and for that reason, I'm not even going to put the dialogue or proceeds of what we talked about in this book.

We consumed more cocaine and drank a few Budweisers. Not American Budweisers—the other ones.

A WhatsApp message from an anonymous number has replied to the one hundred Snapchat, Instagram, iMessage and WhatsApp messages we have sent out asking people "WYS" (what you saying).

The number isn't saved, which means we met them at a club, and the contents and context of the text allude to them most likely being a socialite of sorts.

07767212121: "Come to the Grove now."

Perfect—another shitty night at a club I can't afford. My heart just wasn't in it anymore.

A voice inside said this isn't what it used to be.

The voice inside said, "You've had fun, leave on a high." We put on our jackets and headed out. High.

"When feeling low, leave on a high."

CHAPTER 21

I learnt then that there are some places you go you can't come back from.

The doctor started to connect the dots in his head. I watched him as it unravelled.

"Greeny, black guy, skinny as a stick... he was here today?" he recalled.

"Bingo," I replied; this was the kind of place he would go. I watched his face as he connected the dots.

...

I continued as he spaced out:

"So anyway, the way I saw it, I had two options:

GET A JOB OR FLEE THE COUNTRY.

- Naturally, I thought of fleeing the country as a rational first option.
- • However, in order to flee the country, I needed to get a second vaccine, which I could not legally do until four weeks passed.
- So I tried a few jobs; I even tried the old playgrounds like the Square, Elizabeth's, and a shitty little joint near Great Portland Street run by a skinny, ugly fella that had a thing for giving underage girls too much alcohol.
- I learnt something profound working at every single one. I thought creative directors were bad. That was until I met Mayfair club managers.
- Club managers are the boss level of shitty people; they're drug-addicted miserable perverts.
- Sure, that was harsh, and I'm sure they're not all like that; I'm sure some of them are lovely, but I know for a fact the four I met aren't.
- After a trial shift at a small shitty joint near Great Portland Street run by a thirty-five-year-old pervert,
- I got a night shift working at The Cuckoo Club.

- Nine p.m. to eight a.m. Fifteen pounds an hour to pour rich Russian, Arab and European heirs and heiresses alcohol.

The upside to working at a place like this is that you can get a lot of cash tips, you only have to work two days a week, and it will deter you from drinking, doing drugs or wanting to have sex ever again.

There I am, standing in my cute little busboy outfit, trying my best to be charming, failing miserably as my fake smile comes off as borderline psychopathic.

When a skinny, balding Swedish man tries to use my face for stabilisation.

I promptly remove his hand from my face and place it on the wall next to me. He mumbled something that wasn't "I'm sorry" and then handed me ten pounds in cash to pour him a drink.

I happily picked up someone else's, took a reverse sip directly in front of his inebriated face and handed it to him.

None of this bothered him. This didn't bother me, either.

Anyhow, this inebriated Swedish bloke then proceeded to hit on a Russian girl who was probably around twenty. Everyone in this club is either twenty to thirty or thirty to sixty.

Cuckoo has perfectly hit a demographic of individuals with no idea what a good club is like.

Anyhow, I carried on watching the Swedish man attempt to chat up this girl. He tried all the table club tricks; he got me to pour her a drink and then tipped me handsomely whilst exposing his rose gold Audemars Piguet watch. I knew it was worth two hundred thousand.

She was not impressed.

He ordered a bottle service show; the bottles of Dom came out held by strippers and illuminated by cheap sparklers.

She was not impressed.

He ordered another magnum of what he thought was Grey Goose, but I knew it to be Smirnoff (I had poured Smirnoff and water into all of these bottles four hours prior).

She was still not impressed.

He was scared, terrified even, of this tiny little blonde Russian lady who was not impressed in the slightest by any of his grand gestures or advances.

Perhaps there was still a little hope in this world. I carried on watching instead of doing my job.

He scrambled, looking at his friends. They had pulled; he was the last one left; what could he do?

He looked into the emptying club, the sea of people drifting slowly toward the door; he needed to act now.

He pulled out his phone, clicked on his Crypto.com app and showed her his Ether.

I thought to myself, surely not, but then I looked around and knew this would probably work.

They kissed.

I let out a "Fuck; I need more money."

The Swedish guy heard me and took what I said as a compliment.

He looked at me, arm over the girl's shoulder, ready to leave the club, and said confidently,

"You're starting to get it; now get me a drink."

Ren was also working at the club that night. Well, I say working; he was essentially there to get girls' numbers and be generally amusing.

He neglected a Russian oligarch's cup and ended up pouring some gin on his loafers, looking away into the crowd to see if there were any girls he knew walking around.

The Russian complained, and the managers grabbed him by the collar and pulled him upstairs to fire him.

I looked around the club at my fellow busboys, most of them in their late fifties, backs crooked, wearing pink hats, holding inflatable sex dolls, and all beaming from ear to ear as rich cunts throw fives, tens and twenties at them like strippers. Fuck this.

I grab a shot from the table, down it and then down another, and text Ren.

Courtney: You fired?
Ren: 'Bout to be.
Courtney: How are you texting me then?
Ren: Not paying attention, the fella's geared up, chatting shit.
Courtney: Imma quit. Be up in a sec.

I throw my apron at the head of the inebriated Swedish bloke who tried to use my head for stabilisation and walk up the back room stairs to the office.

The walls are stained with sticky liquids and gum, lots of fucking gum; I can hear inaudible shouting going on upstairs.

No doubt Ren is getting it from a fat, geared-up, inebriated manager. I turned the corner, went down some stairs, and then up some stairs. What I found was far better.

Ren was screaming at the manager.

"YOU FUCKING FAT DRUG-ADDICT PERVERT, LOOK AT YOU, PATHETIC, YOU WANNA FIRE ME?!"

Ren towered over him.

"YOU WANT TO FIRE ME?" he repeated, banging on his chest. The manager was shocked.

Ren edged closer to him, slowly, real slow, so slow that each move forward gave the implication that when he reached his target, violence was guaranteed.

"You little twer—"

"GIVE ME MY FUCKING MONEY THEN!" Ren interrupted, screaming into his face.

The manager scanned Ren, and I'm sure he asked himself, could I win? If it came to blows, could I win?

Ren edged closer and let the silence fortify his anger.

Every time the manager was about to open his mouth, he moved closer.

"All right, I'll give you your money in cash." He raised his hands peacefully.

I chimed casually behind, "Um, and mine too, please."

He walked over to a cash counter and began to count our money.

"You two are charmless," he said, holding the last small bit of authority over us in his hands.

I snatched it from him.

"Good day... sir." I smiled charmingly.

We stuffed the cash in our pockets, grabbed our jackets, ran downstairs, took some free shots from a nearby table, and I accidentally used the Swedish guy's head as a stabiliser really quickly, with a closed fist.

We emerged from the humid club air and into the dark, packed, cold London streets.

Ren headed to a party, so we said our goodbyes.

I walked down the road to Piccadilly Circus, where the big statue is, and sat down, defeated.

A digital billboard with a Nike advert keeps taunting me. "Just do it."

"I'm fucking trying," I replied.

"Can I have a cigarette, please?"

A homeless fella asked, sitting next to me.

Usually, I'd move, but fuck it, we both smelt like a distillery, and you know what? Maybe I'd get some good karma from this.

I opened a pack of Benson & Hedges and offered him one. "What a treat."

"First time I've heard that about B&H."

This was a low; I mean, this was a real fucking low, smoking B&H at six a.m. with a homeless bloke after getting fired.

I looked at him; his face was covered in tattoos, his hat covered in pigeon shit, and his hands calloused and hardened.

If anyone has a temporary solution to this problem, it's this guy.

"Shot in the dark here, but do you know any bars or casinos open around here?"

The homeless fella smiled, revealing a set of gold and yellow teeth.

He pointed straight ahead toward Soho, then right, then down, then right, and then finally, he gave me the thumbs up.

"You got like a name or something I can Google?"

He shook his head and held out his hand.

"Fair." I handed him a twenty from the cash I got from the club and crossed the street.

"Down the street, take a right, take a right, then down, then right, and then you're there."

I repeated over and over again in my mind.

The first street was covered in happy-ending places.

"Vanilla, Jasmine, Mint, Jasmine Mint... Tropical, that's new."

I'd never had a tropical happy ending before, but I assume it would be relatively similar to a happy ending, but the rooms are hot, or maybe they have plants inside.

Stay focused, Courtney.

Down the second street, a couple of homeless fellas were getting off, smoking some crack and drinking K ciders.

Another right.

A couple more homeless fellas, a couple of happy-ending places, a tanning salon, and a sign pointing to a hatch that leads to an underground passage.

I looked around and then went down the empty passage. Fuck it; I gave that guy a twenty.

At the bottom of the hatch was a tiled street.

It dawned on me that this must be an abandoned train station.

On the left was a store called WE LOVE HATS?; directly opposite it was a store called DECENT HATS.

The owners were nowhere to be seen.

I think I'd rather buy a decent hat than buy one from someone unsure whether they LOVE HATS or not.

But that's just me.

At the end of the passage, about five stores down on the right and five doors down on the left.

I could see it.

Its name is in big gold writing:

OF COURSE, PADDY'S

A twenty-four-seven Irish bar, the last of its kind.

Outside the old hidden pub, two tired-looking chefs sat outside sitting on food crates playing cards and drinking half-pints of Guinness.

"Half-pints of Guinness?" I stated inquisitively.

They looked up at me and gave me the thumbs up whilst scowling.

I took this as an order to look up instead of an answer to my question.

So I looked up, and next to the large PADDY'S on the front of the door, wrote: "WE DO VACCINES."

There it was; karma had done me a solid.

I looked at the chefs and then back at the sign. "OF COURSE, PADDY'S do vaccination shots?"

The large one on the right put his cards down and said in a wispy French accent, "That's Doctor Paddy to you."

I smiled and walked in, and that's how I got here.

THE END

Printed in Dunstable, United Kingdom

63487377R00127